PANKRATION

In memory of SGS Francis Borgia Egan,

who taught me more than any other teacher.

Carpe diem! she said, and I did.

Remembered with gratitude and affection

PANKRATION

DYAN BLACKLOCK

A LITTLE ARK BOOK

ALLEN & UNWIN

First published in 1997 by
Allen & Unwin Pty Ltd
9 Atchison St, St Leonards, NSW 1590 Australia
Phone: (61 2) 8425 0100
Fax: (61 2) 9906 2218
E-mail: frontdesk@allen-unwin.com.au
URL: http://www.allen-unwin.com.au

10 9 8 7 6 5 4 3 2

National Library of Australia
cataloguing-in-publication entry:

Blacklock, Dyan, 1951- .
Pankration.

ISBN 1 86448 295 8

I. Title.
A823.3

Designed by Sandra Nobes
Cover illustration by Peter Gouldthorpe
Typeset by Midlands Typesetters
Printed by Australian Print Group, Victoria, Australia

ACKNOWLEDGEMENTS

There were many moments during the writing of *Pankration* when I needed expert medical advice. For this I turned to Dr Mark Crawford, my favourite GP, who, unfazed by questions such as 'What would happen if you got stabbed through the hand?', cheerfully involved himself in the creative act. My grateful thanks to Dr Mark. Thanks also to my mother, Frances, who read the first draft and offered many constructive criticisms. To my editor, Sarah Brenan, I owe my warm thanks for her patience and perception.

Many people have wondered how to pronounce 'Pankration'. We can't know for sure how the ancient Greeks would have said it, but I say 'Pan-krat-ee-on'.

PROLOGUE

The sun had barely risen, and already the air rising from the cobblestones of the agora was hot enough to hide from. Despite the heat, the marketplace hummed with life. Stall-holders setting up grumbled about the blistering day ahead—and about the shortages, the war with Sparta, the overcrowding, what the politicians had said or done. Passers-by called out greetings. Flies buzzed and settled.

Myron, the sweet seller, wiped away the sweat running down his face and sighed. Who would want sweets on a scorching day like this? Everyone would be looking for something cool to drink, and he had nothing in that line to sell. He continued to lay out his trays of honeyed cakes and figs in syrup and fat candied almonds, as he had done every morning for thirty years. No point in complaining, the day

7

would just go slower if he did.

A sudden thump on the linen canopy above his head made him look up, and he saw the unmistakable indent of a small, heavy creature. He walked out into the open to see what it was, and froze. He was staring straight into the eyes of a rat.

Myron had been afraid of rats since he was a child; their keen yellow teeth, pointed grey ears and whip tails terrified him. He screamed and hit out with his staff. The cart tumbled over and food scattered across the cobbled stone roadway, but by a lucky accident the cart handles pinned the rat's head to the ground. Myron whacked the rat several times to make sure of killing it and prodded the body with his foot. Then he set his cart to rights, picked up the food and went on selling all through the rest of that stifling day.

The afternoon shadows lay in long, dull ribbons over the agora as he packed up his cart, and made his slow way home. Perhaps if he'd known he would never walk that way again, he might have stopped and looked at everything more closely, enjoying the walk; but few men ever know when they are about to die.

Myron's house was cool, and almost bare of furniture. He had never married, so he had no need to spend his hard-earned money on household comforts. There was a rug he'd got in exchange for a large debt owed him by the fat carpet-seller in the agora—a small bowl with red and black figures dancing across it, which held his porridge in the morning—and very little else. On the rug was his bed, a thick pallet of straw, exactly to the liking of fleas. He had brought some new fleas home tonight, but he didn't notice. Night was often one long itch for Myron.

The fleas from the rat he had killed bred quickly and by morning some were already laying eggs among the fibres of his rug. He was covered in red, itchy lumps when he woke up. It made him irritable and his head ached. The thought of another day in the sweltering sun trying to sell his wares was more than he could stand, so he decided to stay at home. The next day, and the next, were even hotter, and Myron felt weak and faint. He scratched himself endlessly. On the morning of the third day, for the first time since he could remember, Myron was too sick to get up.

A week later he died. His family performed the burial rites, and removed the rug, the bowl, the chickens and the dog.

Soon the first of Myron's relatives was dying.

CHAPTER

1

An unnatural silence, like the absence of crickets in summer, filled the house.

Nicasylus sat on a couch in the dim, cool men's quarters and thought about running outside into the hot street to join the other boys. He wished he had something to help pass the time; anything would be better than waiting, the way he had been, for hours.

Upstairs, Artemis was cutting off her beautiful hair. He couldn't imagine his sister gone any more than he could imagine her hair cut off. She was only two years older than he, but she sometimes seemed more like his mother than his sister. The things Nic would miss most were the honey cakes she cooked, better than anything you could buy in the agora, and the way she played her flute. On nights when there was no moon, he often lay in the dark listening to the soft, melodic sounds that floated down from the womens' quarters. Would she keep her long black plait, he wondered, or let it be swept up from the floor like rubbish? Nic scuffed his sandals on the stones. He felt like a child again, the way he had when the news of Father's death came. He wanted to cry, he wanted to shout; but there was no way to hurry this process—it had its own rhythm—hair cutting, ritual bath in holy water, anointing with oils, putting on the gold brooches made by Gorgias, their stepfather, for her dowry. Tonight would be the last time Artemis ate with the family. Later tonight Pittacus would come to claim her as his wife.

Pittacus. How *could* Gorgias have chosen him as Artemis's husband? The man made Nic's skin crawl. He was at least thirty—twice Artemis's age; a coarse, ugly man who only wanted a silent wife to bake his bread and clean his house, make and mend his clothes. And she had better bear him strong sons, not any useless girl children. Pittacus would have the female infants thrown out on the rubbish tip to die.

Nic sighed. It was no use thinking these thoughts. That's how life was for women. He wandered into the courtyard. Usually he liked to throw rocks at the chickens, making them squawk and run. Tonight they scuttled at the sound of his feet on the stones and he was left with just the old sow, who didn't move for anyone. The household shrine was laden with fresh flowers and fragrant leaves in honour of the impending

12

marriage, and in the pit, a fire was burning—he could smell the sweet flesh of a young goat roasting. He sat down heavily on a seat by the well. Artemis always complained about that well. She'd have preferred to walk to the fountain house in the agora.

'Better to walk and carry the water home, than be locked inside all day,' she always said. 'At least I'd get to talk to other women there.' Well, Artemis would get her wish soon enough. Pittacus had no well in his house.

Tears sprang up in Nic's eyes. The unfairness of it all offended him. Artemis was pretty and clever, she was funny and smart and the best cook in the world; she'd be wasted on that pig of a man. Nic was selfish enough to want his sister here at home, where she belonged. He'd miss her more than he wanted to think about; except for her, he had no real company at home. The slaves didn't really count, and anyway their work kept them so busy that he hardly saw them. Gorgias spent all his time in the agora, selling silver and gold jewellery to rich men. He loved to debate with the philosophers there, sometimes staying so long that the family barely saw him at all. Nic had noticed that even when Gorgias was home, he avoided spending time with Mother. Or perhaps it was the other way around—Mother avoided Gorgias.

Since Father had died in the war with Sparta, Mother had become a gentle shadow of herself. All her old passion and life had withered like grapes on the vine at the end of summer. She was neither loving, nor unloving. Instead it felt as though the woman he had once known was suspended at some dreadful, dead midpoint between the two emotions. She was still efficient—the household ran smoothly and there was no argument or anger—but Nic often thought it would have been better if home *were* more fiery. Anything would have been preferable to the elegant, ordered quiet and the absolute lack of any kind of excitement.

He heard the sound of feet on the stairs, lethargic and heavy. They were coming down together.

'Nicasylus.' It was his mother who spoke. 'It is time for the meal.' He nodded and tried not to stare at Artemis; already she looked so very different.

The meal was a celebration. Everything was delicious. He wished he had a better appetite to do justice to such a feast, but even though Artemis pressed him to take a bite of the tender kid and dipped his bread in the rich sauce, he could not enjoy his food. He ate a few figs and a little cheese, and kept silent. Artemis tilted his chin with her finger.

'Why so quiet, my little sparrow? Cheer up.'

Tears threatened to splash down Nic's cheeks the way they had when he was just a baby.

'I don't want you to go, Artemis,' he tried not to cry. 'I can't bear it if you leave.'

Gorgias spoke quietly from his couch.

'You must be a man about this, Nicasylus. Your

14

sister has to marry and Pittacus will provide well for her. These pleas are unnecessary.'

Mother said nothing. She stared at her plate of food, which had barely been touched, and would not join in the discussion at all.

'Only miss me when I'm gone, eh?' Artemis smiled and made an effort to keep her voice light-hearted, but Nic could tell that she wanted to cry too. 'You'll have to find a slave who can play the flute or sing you songs to make you sleep, instead of me. Come on, Nic. I need a happy thought to take with me tonight.' Nic could feel her tremble. He straightened his back. He had to be brave, for her sake. After all, it was not he who would soon be carried off by the loathsome Pittacus.

He thought of the huge, hoary toads that sat like lumps of slime on the edge of swamps, swallowing down the beautiful summer damsel-flies. Pittacus was a toad, Artemis was a damsel-fly, and tonight she would be swallowed up by that dreadful creature.

It was dark when he heard the sound of the chariot and the noisy, coarse laughter of Pittacus and his friends outside. His stepfather went to greet the guests and his mother silently left the room—perhaps to send slaves carrying the dowry to the bridegroom's house. This was the worst night of her daughter's life, but if she cared she certainly didn't show it—didn't kiss her

15

daughter or offer advice or comfort. Artemis sat still as a stone, the smile dying on her face.

Pittacus had crossed the threshold of the house and stood with his feet splayed like a duck, his belly stuck out in front of him. Spots of grease from his dinner stained his robe.

'Not even the grace to put on something clean,' thought Nic, and he turned to his sister. She stared at the floor, a blank look on her face. He couldn't bear it. He wanted to shout and push Pittacus and all his horrible friends back out the door, but he didn't. Instead he put his arms around Artemis and buried his face in her dress.

'Goodbye,' he mumbled, 'I'll miss you.' She touched his face with her soft hand, kissed him and was gone. The sound of the chariot and the men faded into the night.

In the morning, the house was busy. Nic woke, stretched himself, and for a few seconds he forgot that Artemis was gone. Then it came back with a sickening rush. How was she feeling right now? He didn't really want to think about it.

The morning meal was late, which was unusual. The slave who usually carried in the tray of food never showed up at all; instead, the old woman who washed the clothes brought breakfast in to him. She muttered

16

as she walked and her hair hung around her face in knotty strands.

'Where's the girl who usually does this?' Nicasylus demanded.

'Dead.' The old woman's eyes looked wild, and she hurried out again without any further explanation. Nic stared at his plate; there was no bread on it, only some fruit, and beside it a jug of water. He was hungry, no dinner last night left him with an empty belly this morning. He picked up the fruit and ate it as he made his way to the kitchen.

The household was in an uproar. Instead of the usual quiet, efficient order, there was chaos. His mother looked distracted when he found her.

'Where's my bread?' he demanded petulantly. 'I'm hungry, and there was no bread on my plate this morning.'

'You'll have to find it yourself, Nicasylus,' she answered him. 'Two of the slaves died last night. I have my hands full arranging for them to be prepared for burial.'

'Died?' he was astonished. 'Two of them? Was there a fight? What happened?' His mother ignored the question.

'Get the bread yourself, Nicasylus. I don't have time to discuss anything with you right now.' She bustled out of the room and he was left to get himself ready for school, an unheard-of event. Where was the slave

17

who went with him? What was going on? There was plenty of bread in the kitchen, but it was stale. No one had baked this morning. Nic chewed each mouthful slowly and carefully as he dressed. He didn't like this one little bit—it was as if he had been completely forgotten.

The slave who eventually appeared looked white and frightened.

'What's going on around here, Phidolas?' Nic demanded angrily. 'Why are you taking me to school? This isn't your job. Where's Milo?' He knew he sounded like a child, but he didn't care; really this was too much. If only Artemis had been here, *she* would have answered all his questions.

'There's a terrible sickness in the slave quarters, master.' Phidolas trembled and his voice was shaky. 'It's killed two and there's one more who looks as if he has it.'

'What kind of sickness?' Nic was astonished. All the slaves were well treated. He could not imagine what would make two of them die overnight.

'No one knows, master.' The slave was clearly frightened. 'But they say that in Piraeus many are already dead. And they die in agony.'

'How?' Nic was inclined to think Phidolas was exaggerating all this.

The slave's eyes widened. 'First their eyes turn red, their skin burns and they bleed from the throat and

18

tongue. They have pustules everywhere that weep a sticky liquid and soon they lose control of their bowels. They get a terrible thirst that drives some to jump into any water they can find. They act like madmen. Then they die.' The simple way the slave said all that, and the look of absolute terror on his face, was enough to make Nic afraid too.

'Have you seen this yourself?'

'Yes.' Phidolas nodded his head vigorously. 'And I've heard it's all through the huts along the road from the port as well. So many people are dying that it is impossible to bury them all. There is a plague in Athens, master.'

'Rubbish.' Nic said it with more conviction than he felt. 'It's just some fever, or a minor illness among those filthy refugees. A few people dying doesn't mean a plague. You're exaggerating.'

They walked to school without exchanging another word. Nic didn't want to hear any more. Anyway, a few slaves dying wasn't the end of the world. His step-father could just buy some more.

CHAPTER

2

Nothing had really been the same after Father died. Women without the protection of a man were considered dangerous, so widows had to marry again immediately and it had to be a relative from the father's family. Gorgias, a distant cousin of Nic's father, was quiet and pleasant enough, and left Nic pretty much alone most of the time. Jewellery was his obsession. Hours could go by while he tapped and teased sheets of gold and molten pools of the precious metal into rings and necklets and earrings. He produced fabulous baubles in his workshop; sparkling, unique jewellery that brought wealthy men from cities far away to buy things for spoiled wives and mistresses.

At first Gorgias had made exquisite things for his new wife. She'd accepted the extravagant gifts, but she never wore any of them. Rubies and emeralds, encased in gold, lay in a drawer like the dead eyes of exotic creatures. It hurt Gorgias, anyone could see that, but he had never said a word. He seemed to know that there was no way he was ever going to replace his cousin, either as a husband or a father.

Plenty of other boys were in the same situation as Nic. Heroic men, who died gloriously in battle against Sparta, had left many widows and fatherless children. Nic knew some boys whose stepfathers had actually left their own families in order to inherit the land and goods of the new wife. At least his own stepfather wasn't a greedy man. He hadn't left another family. He'd come forward to do his duty free of any other ties, and he was generous and thoughtful. There was nothing really to complain about, but Nic still longed for the old days, when his father would come home and grab him in a happy hug, toss him in the air and wrestle with him until he was breathless. Now, with Artemis gone, Nic felt truly alone.

The walk to school took them through the agora, and Phidolas seemed anxious. Nic decided that if there was a plague, then it was probably confined to the port. Most of the usual stallkeepers were in the marketplace, and the philosophers still stood and talked to the young men. Maybe the sickness in his own household was just an unusually fierce one. Anyway, he forgot about it as soon as he got to school. Everything there was normal.

It was all very different as they walked back home again a few hours later. In the agora a man was lying dead on the ground. A doctor had stopped to examine the corpse, but nearby the sellers were frantically packing up their goods. The looks on their faces said it all.

'Keep going, master.' Phidolas's voice was shaking. 'Don't stop, don't even look at the man. He's got the plague!' Nic could smell the sweet stink of death in the air. It clogged his nose and throat and made him want to retch in the gutter. Others had already done so.

Somehow he kept his food down. He let the slave hurry him past the dead body without a single backward glance.

At home, things were worse. His mother was flushed, the house was noisy and absolutely stank. Someone had shat on the courtyard floor, and although the mess had been cleaned up there was no disguising the smell. A female slave was wandering glassy-eyed around the kitchen. She was crying out for water, which his mother was trying to help the poor creature to drink. The sight of his ordered, quiet house in this terrible uproar made Nic's flesh crawl. A cold finger of fear settled on his neck.

It was an enormous relief when Gorgias suddenly strode through the front door and took charge.

'Nicasylus, go to your room and stay there until I tell you otherwise.'

Nic went without a word. He couldn't remember ever feeling so frightened.

Gorgias began barking orders at everyone—he made the sick slaves stay in their quarters, and barred them in when they tried to wander through the house in their demented state. As soon as the household had quietened down a little, he called Phidolas and Nic out into the courtyard.

'Phidolas, I want you to pack a bag with clean clothes and food for yourself and Nicasylus,' he said calmly. 'And hurry.' The slave was gone in a moment. 'I'm sorry, but there is no possibility of you staying here in Athens, Nic. This plague is burning a path through the entire city.' Gorgias looked tired. 'I've sent a message by carrier pigeon to my brother Diagoras, in Argos. He is expecting you.'

Everything was suddenly moving too fast for Nic. He opened and shut his mouth but nothing came out. The slave reappeared with a bundle under his arm.

'You will take my son to Piraeus,' Gorgias said to Phidolas, 'and with him, board a boat for Argos. Make your way to the house of my brother, Diagoras, in the city there. Anyone will direct you. Stay with him until I send for you both.' He pressed a purse full of silver drachmas into the slave's hands and looked hard at Nic. 'Do as Diagoras tells you and try not to make yourself a nuisance.'

Nic felt as if he were inside a funnel, sliding crazily

downwards without any sides to grip. It occurred to him that he had never heard Gorgias call him 'son' before. Somehow it made the whole insane scene even more frightening.

'You two must hurry. This is a plague worse than any I have seen before.' Gorgias slipped a small gold ring, engraved with the face of Athena, off his own little finger and handed it awkwardly to Nic. 'I meant to give you this later. It is my gift to keep you safe.' Nick stared. The ring had been on his stepfather's finger since the day he had come into the house. Gorgias never took it off.

'Your mother is with the infected slaves,' Gorgias clenched and unclenched his fists in a nervous gesture. 'I've tried to get her to leave them. I'm afraid she will catch this disease too, but she insists on looking after even the sickest. She'll see you in a few months' time when this has passed, and says until then, to remember she loves you and wishes you a safe journey. As do I. The gods be with you both.' He looked embarrassed. Almost roughly, he pushed Nic and the slave through the open door. 'Be on your way,' he said gruffly and gave a short wave. The ornate wooden door slammed in their faces.

The whole way to Piraeus there were fires, and palls of black smoke hung in the air. Athens was burning its dead. Nic was glad of the cart that took them the few kilometres to the busy port. The day had been long and frightening, and now, bumping along on his way out of the city, he felt the loss of all that was normal and secure. He had never been outside Athens in his life. Now he was going to board a boat and sail to the distant city of Argos, where he would depend on a relative he had never met to take care of him. There was every chance he would never see his own family again. Who would look after his sister? The thought of Artemis with only Pittacus to protect her terrified Nic more than anything else.

The walls between the port and Athens flashed past. The ring on his finger felt new and out of place, and he twisted it back and forth as he tried to imagine what was going to happen. What would Argos be like? Was Diagoras a kind man? Had they managed to leave in time, or were they carrying the plague with them? It was enough to scramble his brain. When the cart stopped at the entrance to the boat harbour, he felt more anxious and confused than he had ever been in his life.

'This way, master.' Phidolas led the way to where a ship lay waiting. The wharf was cluttered with baskets and bales and strange packages ready to be loaded onto the cargo boats that waited all around them.

'Don't eat much, if you want to be comfortable on the journey. Too much food in your gut now will only end up on the deck later.' The slave laughed, but Nic grimaced and put away the meat he had been about to eat. Phidolas began talking to the captain of the craft, a huge man called Gellius, who seemed to think the journey to Argos should take them about ten hours; even less if the winds were fair. They would thread their way first through the Gulf of Saronikos, and then up the gulf of Argolis, to the very top; there, according to Gellius, Argos sat like a jewel in the landscape. He stowed their goods and showed them where they could lie down. It was a narrow space among the cargo, but Nic immediately dropped down onto the floor. It was not very comfortable, and for a moment he wished he had his own bed to lie on; then he thought of the nightmare-house he had left, and the cargo hold seemed suddenly a lot better. There were still a couple of hours left before the ship would sail, the captain told them.

'I'm going to stay here for a while, Phidolas,' Nic said. 'I really need a rest.' He fell into a deep, dreamless sleep.

When he woke, the whole ship was rocking—they must have set sail already. Nic hurried up to the deck, angry with the slave for not waking him when the first ropes were cast off so that he could watch his homeland fade from sight. What he saw, however, made his grievances evaporate like mist.

The boat was in full sail, skimming quietly across the water. An enormous harvest moon lit the sea like a lantern, outlining the land but showing no detail. The warm scent of the ocean on the summer wind, the soft creaking of the timbers, the moonlight—this was certainly different from Athens. The heat of the city was gone; instead there was a wonderful, fresh sea smell, and for the first time Nic felt excited by the prospect of the trip ahead. He picked his way over the ropes and baskets that littered the deck, and almost tripped over the nearly naked body of the captain.

'Watch out!' The captain rolled himself back onto his haunches, his muscled body gleaming from the perspiration that ran freely over his skin. 'You nearly flattened me while I had my nose to the boards, boy!' His laugh was infectious, and Nic found himself more amused than embarrassed. The man went back to doing push-ups, very fast, sometimes with just one arm supporting his body while the other lay behind his back. His legs and arms were massive and the muscles of his back rippled in the moonlight. He had done so many that Nic lost count, when on some invisible signal, he leaped to his feet with one huge spring, his hands flying above his head in a triumphant V.

'There. Do I look like a champion?' he demanded. 'Next year, boy, you can come to Olympia and watch me win the olive crown for Athens.' He straightened his tall frame and looked up at the sail above his head. 'I will have my statue made by Phidias himself when I win.'

'What sport do you compete in?' Nic asked. 'Wrestling? Running?'

'Hah! Sports that may be good for some, but not for me. I will compete in the Pankration.'

Nic stared. The Pankratiasts were the best of the best—the strongest, fiercest men. They, more than any other contestants at the Olympic Games, were prepared to die for their sport.

'Aren't you afraid?' he blurted out. He had heard lots of tales about these men and their vicious sport. Contestants in the Pankration fought bare-fisted and without weapons, but a contestant could trip the other man up, sit on him, stamp him with his feet or kick him; deliberately dislocating fingers, arms or ankles was not an uncommon way to win a match. No points were awarded for clever moves or good blows, success only came from an opponent surrendering because the pain was too great.

'You had better not enter the Pankration afraid,' said the captain. 'To win you must be brave above all, as well as strong, and flexible like a reed in the wind. It's no good being big and muscular and not being able to jump out of the way or slip from your opponent's grasp.' Gellius spun his giant body and dipped and twisted like a feather on the only tiny square of deck that was free of sailing gear. 'See?' he laughed out loud.

Nic liked his laugh, he'd never met anyone who laughed the way Gellius did. It was as if he were a child, and not a man at all.

'I'd like to go to Olympia one day,' he said hesitantly. 'My father went once. He competed in the Hoplite Race.'

'Ahh! A man strong enough to race in full battle dress! He must be quite a man.'

'He died four years ago.' Nic stared at the sea, trying to keep the tears from falling. It would be so embarrassing to cry. Gellius followed his gaze, not looking at Nic's face.

'My father was also a soldier,' he said softly. 'And when he died and my new father came, I thought I'd never recover from my grief. I cried myself to sleep for three years.' He slapped at the rail with one huge hand. 'But I grew up, boy, as you are doing. I discovered I loved the sea better than anything else, and I've sailed it for the past ten years as master of my own boat. All that time I've sweated and trained, and I've saved enough to pay my way to Olympia, so next year I'm going, come tempest or high water. See that?' He pointed to the giant golden globe above them. 'That's an Olympic moon. This time next year, as that moon rises over the horizon, I'll be in the *Altis* at Olympia, lighting a sacrificial fire to honour the gods—to thank them for my win. I'll bring the olive crown back to Piraeus for me and my father.'

'I'd like to see that.' The captain's enthusiasm was contagious.

'Well, if you're still in Argos this time next year,

I'll call by and pick you up. If your relative agrees, of course. What do you say? We'll sail to Pirgos and make our way along the river Alpheus to Olympia. You can watch me compete.'

'Definitely. Absolutely!' Nic stuck out his hand.

The two shook hands solemnly.

'You do mean it, don't you?' Nic asked hesitantly. Why should Gellius take such an interest in a boy he had only just met? Maybe he was just being kind and didn't really intend taking him to Olympia.

'It's a promise, lad, and I keep my promises. I'll come for you when the moon is full, in August.' The captain punched Nic lightly on the shoulder. 'And you'd better cheer loudly when I win!'

They stood on the deck for a while longer, talking and dreaming aloud about the following year and all the glory that would belong to Gellius when he won at Olympia. Nic forgot he was with a grown man, and Gellius forgot he was with a boy. They talked until Phidolas appeared and sent Nic below. The boy fell asleep with his mind full of the Games, and in his dreams he could see his real father clapping and cheering as the olive wreath was placed on his head.

'Nic,' his father said, 'this has been the hardest fight of all, and you've won. I'm very proud. You've shown the courage of a man.'

It was a long time before his dream made any sense to Nic.

CHAPTER

3

Above the inky blue waters of the gulf of Saronikos, the white sail of the small wooden trading boat billowed and swelled. A brisk wind had caught it, and was pushing the craft swiftly across the sea towards Argos. It was still dark, but the moon gave a spectacular brightness to everything. Dawn was less than an hour away—already a fine crack of light had pierced that unlit margin between sea and sky.

At the steering oar, a sailor snored gently. It was the last watch of the night. He was tired and the ship seemed to sail herself in these calm waters. The other crew member was fast asleep as well, so it was easy for the pirates to manoeuvre their vessel right alongside and board. They slit the sleeping sailor's throat from ear to ear and took the knife that lay on the deck at his feet. The wooden rattle he had been carving for his new baby son they kicked into the sea.

A soft thump of timber on timber as the two boats rose and bumped together on the swell woke Phidolas. He climbed the ladder to the deck. The slave stuck his head through the hatch just in time to see the knife that lunged at his throat. He had a moment to scream before it struck, and the scream woke Gellius and the first mate, both asleep on the deck as well.

It took Nic a few moments to work out what was happening. He heard the scream and the thud of Phidolas's body falling. It was like a dream, nothing made sense. He could hear shouting and screaming and the sound of men on the deck above. He climbed the ladder, but had the sense to keep his head low and not stick it through the hatch like poor Phidolas, whose bloody body lay in a crumpled heap on the floor. On deck, a mighty fight was taking place. The ship seemed to be swarming with men. Gellius was engaged in deadly hand-to-hand combat with one of them, and Nic could see the other sailor fighting on the port side. He began to climb back down the ladder to find a weapon of some sort, but he had only taken a single step when a dark arm reached from behind and closed around his throat. In a second he was unconscious.

When Gellius saw his young passenger being carried off, he let out a mighty roar. With one huge leap he cleared the distance between himself and the pirate carrying Nic's limp body across his shoulders. The captain's sword swung up in a tremendous arc, but before he could bring it down, a violent shove from behind sent him crashing onto the deck. A knife passed straight through the palm of his right hand and pinned him to the deck as effectively as a fly to a board. Anyone else would have passed out from the pain, but Gellius had trained as a Pankratiast; pain was something he could tolerate better than most men. With his free hand, he grabbed at his assailant's leg, and almost brought him crashing to the deck. The man swore and kicked Gellius hard in the side of the head. Gellius managed to roll sideways as another pirate struck at him, but there was no way he could avoid the blade of a long sword which slid into his side and out again, sticky and red. Gellius felt his eyes widen.

'It doesn't hurt as much as I thought it would, to die,' he thought, as a soft, gentle darkness welcomed him in.

More than four hours later, Gellius came to. His head ached; his hand was covered with sticky black blood and it hurt more than he could believe was possible. Gingerly he raised his head to look about him. His ship was badly damaged; the sail hung in tatters and nothing worth having had been left behind. The pirates could never have anticipated the fight they got;

probably they had expected a clean raid, capturing a few slaves and some useful goods. They must have assumed he was dead—it didn't make sense to leave behind a strong man who could be sold for a good sum. It was even stranger that the pirates hadn't taken his boat and sailed it away with them. Perhaps too many of their numbers had died; Gellius had fought like the Pankratiast he was. There were bodies everywhere, littering the deck, swollen already in the early morning heat.

With his good left hand, Gellius wrenched the knife from the timbers, screaming aloud at the sudden flashing pain. The blade had missed the bones and the main blood vessel to the fingers, but there was a hole as big as a fat, black olive, bloody and mangled. The wound in his side was a lot less damaging than he had thought—the sword had not pierced any of his vital organs, but had passed cleanly through flesh and muscle—but with a wound like this in his hand he was as good as crippled. Gellius swore. Hand or no hand, if he didn't try to follow the pirates, Nic would be lost for good.

Before he could bind his hand he had to wash it in the sea, dangling overboard at a perilous angle to let the waves slap against the gash in his palm. The salt stung and burned as if he'd dipped his hand into hot coals. He did the same with the wound in his side, letting the sea water cleanse it. Counting himself lucky that he hadn't lost more blood, Gellius dragged himself across the deck and slid down the ladder. At the bottom lay the corpse of the slave, Phidolas. He stepped over the body and picked his way through the chaotic mess below deck. Somewhere was a sharp knife and clean linen bandages. Finding what he needed exhausted him.

Gellius cut away at the ragged skin of his wounds with the razor-sharp knife, making the whole area as neat as he could, then grimaced as he pulled the bandage tightly round his hand, using his teeth to help tie a reef knot so it wouldn't unravel. Strips of linen held the wound in his side firmly closed. Gellius pulled himself up on deck, leaving the slave's body where it was. He could not possibly haul the corpse on deck; he'd have to suffer the smell below and get under way.

Now to get his bearings—the boat would have drifted a long way off course since the attack. Gellius stared out at the flat blue sea. There was no sign of the pirate ship.

Most of the pirates in the Aegean came out of the west. He set his course westward, then began the grim task of rolling dead bodies into the sea and washing blood from the deck with salt water, hauled up painfully and awkwardly using a clay pot tied to a rope. Every movement made his hand and side hurt so much it was almost unendurable, and each time he bent

towards the sea the water below threw hot white frag-
ments of light at him, like splinters from a mirror, that
burned his skin and made his eyes smart.

By noon, the wounds were throbbing mercilessly;
the slightest touch on his right hand scorched like fire,
while his side felt open and raw. The more the
wounds hurt, the more he seemed to knock them
against things. He screamed aloud when the wind
caught the sail he had managed to rig up and the oar
swung unexpectedly, smashing against his injured
hand. Just a short while later, as he was ladling fresh
water down his parched throat, the ship suddenly
heaved; Gellius lost his footing on the slippery deck
and careened into the gunwale, opening the wound
in his side again so that it spurted blood like a burst
pipe. His head hit a stanchion and for the second time
he lost conciousness.

Gellius was not ready to die yet; the gods were still
with him. In the blue distance, a speck separated itself
from the horizon; a small fishing boat. The fishermen
had been out all night and they were on their way
home with their catch when they saw Gellius's boat.
In those pirate-infested waters their first instinct was
to keep well away, until they saw how forlornly the
boat bobbed about with no one in sight. If it were
abandoned, the fishermen reasoned, then they could

keep it. That was enough incentive to make them stop and investigate.

They found Gellius slumped on the deck, unconscious. He was so big that they decided against trying to move him. Instead, one man stayed on board while the others tied his boat to theirs, and they towed it home. It took all three of them to carry the huge, unconscious captain off his boat and up the steep hill to the village. It was like lumping a dead ox uphill and they were exhausted when they finally let him down onto a pallet of straw. A young boy watched in amazed silence. Few strangers came to this village, and he'd never seen the equal of this mountain of a man.

'Get Atthis,' barked the oldest of the fishermen, breathing hard. 'Tell her to bring healing potions.' The boy ran off at top speed. The dark brown stain covering the rough bandages on the man's hand and side, and the pallor of his face under the deep head wound, were enough to tell him that the old herbalist had better hurry.

When Gellius awoke, he was in a house he had never seen before, and an old woman was tending his wounds. It hurt so much, he let out a loud and offensive curse. The old crone appeared not to notice. She smiled, showing fewer teeth than a baby, and muttered something unintelligible. An extraordinary smell, at once sweet and yet still with an edge of bitterness, filled the room. In small pots set at each of the corners were bowls of burning herbs.

'What are you doing, old woman?' Gellius couldn't remember when he'd last been tended by a woman, old or young. She said nothing, but lifting his head in her arms and cradling him like a baby, tipped small drops of a bitter liquid down his throat. As soon as the potion had reached his stomach, Gellius fell back into a deep and quiet darkness.

Waking the second time was not as odd as the first; he remembered, more or less, where he was. He could smell herbs again, but this time they were different. Now there was a wonderful, rich, spicy smell that seemed to come from somewhere very close. He opened his eyes slowly and took his time looking about. He lifted his hand to his nose. The smell was coming from an oil that covered his skin.

'Oil of cinnamon,' came a young voice, 'and white poplar. They'll help keep the sickness out of your wounds. You're very lucky.' The voice took on a bragging note. 'Atthis has the best curative oils in the whole of Greece.'

Gellius looked towards the voice. It was a girl of maybe twelve or thirteen—she didn't look any older than Nic—who was sitting on the floor at the foot of his bed.

'And who might you be?' He raised himself up on

38

his good arm and stared down at her. She blushed.

'My name is Penelope,' she said in a haughty voice, 'and it's very rude to stare like that.' She poked her tongue out at him, and Gellius laughed.

'It's even ruder to poke out your tongue at a stranger, young Penelope,' but he was talking to the back of her chiton—she had flounced out of the room.

CHAPTER

4

Nic woke to a much grimmer picture. There were no healers, no pretty young girls, not even a pallet bed for him, no incense and no sweet oils. He woke up in the depths of the black, stinking hold of the pirate ship, which was at that moment trying desperately to evade capture by a trireme belonging to the Athenian navy.

He couldn't see the trireme, but he could hear the shouted orders on deck above him, and the rising panic was obvious.

Nic had never felt so alone in his life. His stepfather would think he had arrived safely in Argos and it would be a long while before he heard otherwise. Phidolas was dead. If Gellius had died too, then there was no one left to tell what had happened to Nic—no one at all.

Every roll of the ship threw him against the sides of

the hold, slamming him against the timbers—hard. With his hands tied behind his back, he could not keep his balance. Helplessness and queasiness and closeness overwhelmed him. Nic was sick, right where he stood, and afterwards he groaned at the thought of the smell staying with him until he could get out of that hole. He tried to keep himself together by thinking of Artemis, but her face kept fading while the face of his dead father grew brighter in its place.

Nic fell asleep in the end, propped up against the side of the boat in an awkward squat. When, finally, someone shook him, his legs had gone to sleep and he felt pins and needles like hot sparks over his skin. He realised that the sailor had come to bring him on deck, even though he couldn't understand a word the man said. Sardinian, he guessed. His legs refused to hold him so he let himself be dragged along, awkwardly.

The light from the man-hole was like an explosion going off in his face. Nic closed his eyes against it and let the pirate push, pull and prod him all the way up the ladder to the deck. It crossed his mind that maybe he was going to be thrown overboard. Shoved down onto the deck, a foot on his back and his face pressed into the planking, Nic could see nothing but the feet of the man in front of him. Curious, he thought as he lay there, there were six toes on the left foot. An order snapped out above his head—what was it? Throw him

41

to the sharks? His mind seemed to be floating in a detached state; not afraid, simply uninterested in the outcome. Six-toes gave him one final prod, and walked away. Then the ropes tying his wrists together were slashed and he was dragged across the deck to a wooden barrel.

When Nic realised what was happening, he laughed out loud. It was such a relief to be given an opportunity to clean off the smell that seemed to have permeated his skin. He climbed into the barrel and scrubbed fiercely at his body, while the crew stood about, staring and laughing rudely. At last, someone tossed him some clothing—ragged but clean—and Nic began to feel more human, even if the salt stung his cuts and dried in a white, itchy crust on his skin. He was on deck, in the fresh air, and that was as much as he needed. It made him feel ridiculously happy to simply breathe in the salt air.

His pleasure was short-lived; the pirate who had dragged him up on deck began to pull him in the direction of the hold again. Nic resisted; he tried using signs to show he would not run away (where was there to go, after all?), but it did no good. He was pushed through the hole back into blackness and the hatch shut over his head. Once again he could see nothing. His vomit still lay there, stinking just as much as it had before. Nic felt like yelling for someone to clean it up, the way he would have done at home.

Pirates were hardly likely to come and swab out the hold for him. Fixing his mind on Gellius helped—no way would a Pankratiast ever give in just because of the smell of vomit. Anyway, Nic reasoned, now at least he was clean.

Sleep came to his rescue; it seemed only a moment before the hatch was flung open again and the white sun flooded into his eyes, making his pupils, grown as large as saucers in the dark, shrink to the size of a flea. The same pirate shouted something at him, presumably wanting to be saved the effort of coming down there and dragging him up. Nic obliged, climbing cautiously to the top.

He stuck his head over the rim of the hatch and blinked into the sun. Six-toes was standing in front of him; his feet on a level with Nic's chin. How toes could look so menacing was a wonder to Nic, but before he could look up, the feet vanished. He could only see the back of the man's head and hear his voice, roughly issuing orders. Six-toes was the captain, Nic was certain of it, but he spoke the language of the other pirates as though it was not his native tongue. His speech sounded raw and different.

There wasn't much time for these thoughts. Nic found himself bundled up against the gunwale like a soft rag, both hands secured to a stanchion with rope. A cloth was tossed over his face and tied at the back of his head, but even without eyes, he could hear the sail being lowered and smell the approach to land.

It was a while, though, before he felt the soft bump as the ship docked against a pier. There was a considerable hum of noise which sounded like a marketplace. Held firmly by the elbow and half dragged down a gangplank to the pier, Nic found himself again on solid land. His legs still felt as though they were at sea and he rocked involuntarily, though the ground, of course, was perfectly still under him. Another hand—whose? Six-toes, he thought—grasped him firmly and began to walk alongside him. Nic stumbled and almost fell, but was hauled up before he could hit the dirt, and yanked hard to rights. They didn't walk far, only a few paces, before he was stumbling up a flight of steps and onto a platform. There his hands were tethered to a post behind him, and he heard the roar of a large crowd. Six-toes spoke into his ear in a voice that sounded Athenian; using perfect Greek. Was Six-toes a Sardinian pirate, or an Athenian?

'I'll have the ring, boy. You'll have no use for it any more.'

He felt the man pulling roughly at the ring that his stepfather had given him as he left Athens. Enraged, Nic struggled to keep the ring on, twisting his finger so that the band jagged across his unyielding knuckle.

'I'd hate to have had to cut your finger off. You wouldn't fetch such a handsome price.' There was the sound of cruel laughter and the ring was wrenched off violently. Nicasylus heard a thump as his captor leapt down from the platform. A few seconds later the blindfold was ripped from his face and Nic found himself in front of a crowd. A man was standing to one side, obviously describing Nic's physical attributes and people were roaring their appreciation of the man's crude wit. Then silence fell. The bidding had begun.

It was the worst kind of shame, to be sold like an animal. Seventy drachmas was the highest bid and Nic had to endure being checked carefully by his new owner. The man reminded him of Pittacus; he was big and fat and his eyes glinted as hard as flint.

'I hope you like a life out of doors,' he said. 'You're a goat herder now, boy.' He spoke a Greek dialect that Nic could understand, and for a wild moment Nic thought about explaining that he was no ordinary prisoner of war to be bought and sold at market, but an Athenian from a good family. 'Load him on!' The household slave, a huge, silent, black man, lifted him onto the waiting cart as if he were no more than a feather. All the hope Nic had clung to faded away.

CHAPTER
5

Nic's skin felt in danger of shaking loose from his bones. The cart he was travelling in rattled him up and down with no rhythm, just a never-ending bumping on the uneven, rock-strewn road. His head ached, as much from the constant noise and dust and jolting as from the anxiety of not knowing where he was going, or what would happen when he got there. The slave who had lifted him into the cart drove without saying a word or even looking at him. A raucous cough racked the man's body and he spat thick wads of mucus over the side of the cart and onto the road. There was no one else in the vehicle; Nic's new master evidently had a more comfortable way of getting home from the agora.

Nic began to cry and once he started, he couldn't stop; the tears felt good. They'd been held back for so long and for so many reasons. Now he wept like a baby. Every so often he tried to wipe his nose with the back of his hand, but the sticky mess just smeared across his knuckles each time. In the front, the black slave showed no sign of having heard or seen. If anything the coughing grew louder.

For a long while the landscape was only a blur, obscured by tears, but his weeping had stopped altogether by the time the cart drew in to the courtyard of his new master's home. A sullen-faced slave marched over and dragged him down roughly—vegetables from the agora would have been treated more gently. Clothes, clean, but made from some coarse cloth, were tossed at him, and he was led to a trough outside, where he thankfully washed off the grime of the journey. A little fruit and some barley gruel was dumped ungraciously in front of him. It was on the tip of Nic's tongue to ask for some bread, but he thought better of it. The slave sat staring at him in a most unpleasant manner. Perhaps silence was a good idea.

He wondered where he was. His new master spoke passable Greek, but other people in the marketplace had spoken an odd, unfamiliar dialect. He didn't recognise the countryside either. He guessed that he was in a Greek colony, probably somewhere in Italy. It was pointless trying to get any information; the rest of the household slaves stared blankly when Nic said anything. Clearly they didn't understand him either. Nic fell asleep on his hard pallet bed as soon as he lay down, exhausted. Not even the snores and grunts of his fellow slaves could keep him awake.

Nic was sent to milk the goats early the next morning—something he did so badly that another slave took pity and silently demonstrated the right way to make the milk squirt into his bowl. Afterwards he was set to work cleaning the pens; it took two hours to muck the straw out and lay clean bedding. The goats had better accommodation than the slaves, he thought angrily. There was a sour, rank smell about the animals that made him feel sick and he hated the task. All the while he worked, he was watched by the unsmiling slave who had met him. Nic had the feeling that he was supposed to help, but he did absolutely nothing. About mid-morning, he pushed a small pouch of food into Nic's hand and indicated a steep, narrow, dirt path that appeared to lead straight up the mountainside. He led the goats out of their pen and smiled, nastily. With a sinking feeling, Nic realised he was expected to take the goats up to the high pastures. He had always been afraid of heights. Ahead of him was a thin ribbon of a path, winding between gullies and chasms that could swallow him up if he made one wrong step. It terrified him, and he couldn't keep that fear from showing on his face. As he set off, he could clearly hear laughter.

48

He could do nothing to keep the goats together or make them stay on the path. They went wherever they liked, exactly like a bunch of unruly children. They appeared to delight in making Nic run after them, shouting and waving his staff in a futile attempt to stop them wandering off. By the time he found the goat herder's hut he was exhausted. The food in his pouch wasn't very filling after such strenuous exercise. Too tired to think, Nic just swallowed it down thankfully.

The goats were munching on the short sweet grass; it made him angry to watch them so mindless and happy. He was by himself, and yet he was a prisoner. If this were Italy he'd never be able to escape. Greece was a long way over the sea, and without a boat, money and food he wouldn't have a chance. Down at the farm were unfriendly slaves who couldn't or wouldn't communicate with him, and at least one who acted as if the only thing that would make him happy would be to see Nic suffer. Rage and frustration welled up in Nic. He thought of his family, and that only made him feel worse. He wanted desperately to shut out everything. As for the goats, let them fall off the stupid mountain for all he cared! He lay down in the hut and went to sleep.

His dreams were full of swords and death and six-toed pirates, and once the face of Artemis drifted past—unreachable. He tossed and turned and cried out

49

like a child, but no mother or sister came to wake him, or comfort him.

The sun dropped behind the peaks, the air chilled suddenly and Nic woke, overwhelmingly hungry again; but he had eaten all his food, and he knew he would have to get the goats down safely and milk them before he could expect to get more. He struck at the creatures bad-temperedly, and shouted the worst abuse he knew, which made him feel slightly better. Tired still after his restless sleep, he stumbled after them as the sure-footed animals trotted back down the mountain path. There was no pleasure to be had from their safe arrival, there was still too much work to be done. All he could think of was food and a bed, and they were hours away yet.

The first months went past like a bad dream. Nic had not been brought up to clean, sweep, look after dirty animals or do any of the other tasks he was set. He was so resentful at first that he made himself unpopular. The others ridiculed his lack of skills. They mimicked him cruelly, laughing when he stumbled over the language or misused a tool. If anyone *had* befriended him, it might have been different, but no matter what he did, Nic was made to feel unwelcome. In the months that followed he made very little effort to fit in.

The first problem was the language; not all the

slaves spoke Greek. It was a constant struggle to understand what was being said, although he knew that he was being made an object of ridicule—especially by the boy Scopas, who remained his worst enemy. Scopas delighted in tripping him up, dropping fresh, wet cow dung on his bed and doing anything else he could think of that might annoy Nic. On a couple of occasions they nearly came to blows, but Nic managed to walk away. He doubted he'd win a fight with the surly slave, who would certainly fight dirty.

Eventually Nic knew enough of the language to get by; he could ration his food so that the meagre provisions lasted for 24 hours; and, after six months or so, he was able to cope with the goats and their steep path. He also learned not to fall asleep while he was on the mountain. He had been exceptionally lucky, really. All that time there had been no real problems with the goats. As the autumn days shortened, however, a half-starved, female wolf came slinking from the uninhabited peaks. The sudden shrill bleat of a nanny goat, pregnant and slower than the rest, was the signal that stampeded the herd. The wolf took food home to her pups that night, and Nic, frightened and shaking, was left to gather up his terrified herd and drive them back down the mountain.

When he returned with one goat missing, Nic was beaten and given no evening meal. He watched the others eat; Scopas smiled sourly and Nic longed to lash out at his hateful face. Later that night, Tiso, the slave who had brought him home from the market, dropped a small lump of cheese and two figs into Nic's lap. He coughed, a loud rattle in his chest, and kept walking. It was clear he wanted no acknowledgment of his gift. Nic stealthily wolfed down the food. It was strange to have found a friend—or at least it seemed that he was a friend—and yet not be able to say anything to him.

Winter followed autumn, and the land changed; the fields lay bare and only the cypress trees kept their foliage. Over the months Nic got used to the routine and the life. There was something almost soothing about the constancy of it. In the slaves' quarters, he was still the one who ran the errands and did the jobs the others didn't want to do, sometimes working long past sundown after getting up at dawn. Tiso was the only slave who was ever nice to him—the gift of food had bound them in an odd way.

Tiso was probably only about twenty-five, but he looked much older. There was a feeling about him of light being slowly snuffed out. He worked like an ox all day long and well into the night; did all the heaviest work, and without help. Nic had never heard him complain about anything—because the man never spoke. No matter what he did, Tiso never gave more than a shy smile or sometimes a nod or a shake of his head. The only sound that ever passed his lips was the rolling, gurgling cough that was his trademark. Nic became obsessed with getting him to talk.

The importance of knowing why Tiso didn't speak grew and grew. In the end he asked Scopas one morning after milking.

'I've never heard Tiso say a word. Why doesn't he talk?'

'You can't talk without a tongue,' Scopas laughed. 'His was cut out.'

'Why?' Nicasylus couldn't keep the shock out of his voice.

Scopas shrugged. 'It happens.' He narrowed his eyes at Nic. 'Why should you care, anyway?'

'Just curious.' A rush of fear sprang through Nic's body. 'I couldn't care less about him.'

The moment passed; Scopas went back to work, but for the rest of the day Nic thought of nothing except Tiso and his missing tongue. He knew, intuitively, that Scopas and Tiso were old enemies, from the way they avoided each other, the strange dance they did around each other if they were in the same room. Nic couldn't imagine what had ever started it, but he was sure Tiso could thrash Scopas if he wanted to, without even getting a sweat up! Scopas had begun to harass Nic at every opportunity. Tiso, if he happened to be there, eyeballed Scopas until he stopped, but it was only ever a brief respite. It seemed to irritate Scopas that he could never make Nic respond by losing his temper. He'd punch Nic as he passed, or tip the food off his plate so it fell in the dirt; a day never passed without him finding a new way of bullying. There was no reason for this behaviour that Nic could figure out. He steadfastly ignored it.

With no reason to enjoy life in the house, Nic looked forward to the long haul up the mountain. His goats were friends; they no longer strayed, but stayed close together, making it much easier to keep them from the wild, steep places where they could be lost forever. After a while he could tell them apart, and he gave them all names. All day long he wandered among them, chattering away, having long, one-sided conversations with each animal in turn as they stood and ate. He had no one else. He helped the first of the females to give birth one night, and as he watched mother licking the tiny newborn and making small noises of delight, Nic realised that he had begun to relish life again.

A goat herder! It could have been a lot worse. Athens had been so cloistered, so boring. Here in this foreign land, despite the fact that he was a slave, he was free in a way he had never been free before. There was always work about the farm each morning, but since he got up long before dawn he could be well away from there by the time the sun rose fully. After a simple breakfast of porridge Nic took his herd to the top of the mountain. From that lofty position he could see the tiny harbour below, spread out before him like a blue jewel. It was a view he never tired of.

As the seasons came and went, thoughts of home began to be fewer and further apart. Nic could see no way of getting back, and he was not at all sure he would find his family alive if he did. By spring, he had been away almost a year. His family would have had trouble recognising him; the boy who had left Athens was now a young man. The steep climb up the mountainside and the swift goats kept him healthy and strong. He took to running up and across the slopes, instead of walking; his feet hardened and his speed and stamina increased.

Alone with his goats on the mountain, Nic could do what he pleased during the day—he was limited only by his own imagination. He made a flute by tying hollow reeds together with grasses and soon taught himself to play. Even though his music was simple, it kept him company and his goats seemed to like it well enough. He learned to whistle too, something Artemis had never been able to teach him in Athens. He also practised every day with different-sized rocks until he had a perfect aim with a slingshot. When he brought down a wild piglet with a single stone, Nic was elated. He carefully removed its skin and cleaned it as best he could, then stretched the skin over a wooden frame he had made. And that was his drum. Now he could whistle, play his flute or rattle away on his drum. Whenever he felt like it, he could jump into the stream that ran down through the mountain pastures and have a swim.

Until the night the wolf returned, he was happy—almost. After that night, nothing was the same.

Nic had been nursing two sick goats, tethered to the hut so he could keep his eye on them. He somehow nodded off for a short while in the early evening, and woke to find the youngest of the two goats gone. The terrain near the hut was very rugged. There were steep clefts between the ridges where rocks tumbled against each other like a giant broken necklace. He had climbed up the highest of these boulders in order to check the surrounding area when he heard a low growl from directly behind him. The way the sound seemed to come from alongside him made Nic panic; he turned to run but lost his footing and slipped—into the crack between two enormous rocks. He was wedged firmly, unable to free himself, his head a mere handspan below the top of the rock.

The wolf must have been very close; Nic smelt the beast before he saw it. It was a smell so like the dogs that roamed the streets of Athens that for one odd moment he was homesick. The growling was directly above him; instinctively he tipped his head to one side, trying to make it lie flat against his shoulder, and at the same instant, the wolf swiped downwards. Nic felt the breeze as its paw swept past exactly where his head had been a second earlier. His whole body began to shake uncontrollably. Then, from far away, came the bleating of the missing goat. The wolf heard it too. Nic heard its paws scratch the rock as it loped away.

Now was Nic's chance. He sucked in his breath, twisted his torso a fraction, braced his arms against the sides then with one herculean effort pushed himself upwards, just a short distance. His knees were bent slightly, and he could feel a thin rock ledge with his foot. If it would stand his weight, he might manage to lever himself towards the surface. Nic closed his eyes and concentrated, ignoring the pain of his arms and legs scraping against the rough surfaces as he dragged himself upwards, centimetre by centimetre, till his nose, then chin, then shoulders were clear.

The faint bleating of the goat echoed in the distance; it was still alive. With one last burst of energy, Nic dragged himself from the cleft in the rock, bloodied and bruised and scratched. He sat for a moment, his head whirling, unable to make up his mind what to do. The sensible thing would be to run back to the rest of the herd and pen them as quickly as he could, but the sound of his lost goat tore at his heart. It would be terrified, smelling the wolf, feeling it close in for the kill.

CHAPTER

6

It took Gellius three months to recover the use of his hand, and another three months to repair the damage that the pirates had done to his boat. He was an excellent patient, and as Atthis was fond of telling him, he had the advantage of being strong and in good health before he was injured. The wound in his hand had been a clean slice through the flesh, leaving the tendons and bones undamaged—a miraculous accident which meant it healed quickly. Within a few weeks, a large scar was all that remained to remind him of where he had cracked his head open. The sword wound in his side proved a little more troublesome. The blade that had cut him must have been filthy. An infection set in, and it took all of Atthis's herbal wizardry to cure the pus-filled sore that festered for weeks.

Gellius took his time with everything. He knew

only too well, even if Atthis had not reminded him every day, that his recovery depended on regaining strength. He convalesced in the sun, soaking up the warmth like a rich man who had no need to work; forcing himself to relax and accept the generosity of the village.

The townsfolk had taken him in as one of their own. Each day a basket of fresh figs, a fish, eggs or a comb of honey arrived at the door of the house. Penelope carried it to the kitchen, signalling her haughty approval of the food with a whisk of her long brown hair. For a month or so, she treated Gellius with a mix of compassion (whenever his wounds were sore and troubled him) or disdain (when he was well and smiling). He laughed at her when she scowled, trying to make her smile. It amused him to see her frown turn to a laugh then back again in moments, as though she couldn't really decide whether to be cross with him or not.

'You're a lot of work, you know,' she scolded, whenever she wanted to see him squirm. He would smile ruefully and acknowledge that the child was right.

Her father, one of the fisherman who had carried Gellius off the boat, spent a lot of time at sea, and her mother was always either cooking or cleaning or tending the animals and the vines. So it fell to Penelope to entertain the stranger from Athens, which she usually did with a very poor grace; though she was intrigued, he knew—once or twice he'd caught her peeping from behind a giant terracotta pot as he woke from a doze in the sun. When he called out, 'I can see you, Penelope!', she'd leap to her feet and run away inside the house. Next time she appeared she would pretend she hadn't ever spied on him at all. It was a game they played together, and gradually the two of them became friends. Gellius would entertain Penelope for hour after hour, telling tales of his life at sea; of pirates and passengers, fish and foe, storms and shipwrecks. He told her about his dreams of being an Olympic champion, and scared her with fierce and bloodthirsty stories about the Pankration. Inevitably the discussion would turn to Nic. She had to know everything there was to know about the boy. She worried constantly about the awful things that might have happened to him. It was Penelope who insisted that it was Gellius's duty to go back to Athens as soon as he was well enough, and let Gorgias know of Nic's capture. This had already occurred to Gellius, but the very thought of it filled him with dread. How could anyone tell a man that his only son had been taken by pirates; most likely sold into slavery, the gods only knew where! But in his heart, he knew that there was no alternative.

He began to use his hand again as soon as he could: stacking wood, mending the nets, doing the hundred-and-one small things that needed attention around the house. Gellius made himself useful to everyone, since

61

everyone had helped in his recovery in one way or another. When at last he walked down to the harbour to inspect his damaged boat, he found it had already been hauled into dry dock and repairs had begun. He felt an immense gratitude. He had never known such generosity as he'd found in this poor fishing village.

Rebuilding was slow; the seasoned timbers he needed were in short supply in the tiny port. One of the fishermen offered to make a special trip to purchase what he needed, and the entire transaction took place without exchange of money, only promises. No one seemed to mind. The sailmaker in the village supplied a new sail without Gellius paying him a coin. The carpenter repaired all the smashed hatches and woodwork on board, and asked for nothing in return. The ship began to spring back to life again. Within a few weeks she was seaworthy and ready for a test voyage.

The day they launched her, Gellius sailed out between the fishing boats, boosted by a mighty wave of encouragement and a great cheer from the people lining the shore. It felt good to be at the wheel again after so many months on dry land, and neither his hand nor his side gave him any trouble at all. Standing proudly on deck, with a couple of fishermen nearby to help manage the sail and haul on the anchor rope, Gellius took one turn round the harbour; then, with a light breeze in the rigging, he sailed out to sea.

Every part of him felt alive again. Salt air and blue sky and the spray from the bow wave, these were the things he had missed. The men had brought a jug of wine, and there were so many toasts to his boat and his friends that his head began to spin. Eventually they anchored in a small cove where he stripped naked, swam, fished and played the fool with his crew, until reluctantly, as the sun began to set, they sailed home again. Penelope was jumping about on the jetty, grinning and waving like a crazy doll, as they sailed in. She looked so young and vulnerable with her brown hair flying loose she made him think of Nic. He wondered, as he had not let himself wonder since the day he was brought onto the island, what had happened to the boy. The pirates would have sold him in the nearest slave market, probably somewhere on the coast of Italy. He could only hope that whoever had bought Nic was kind. He prayed to the gods that the boy would be well treated.

When Gellius fell asleep that night, his dreams were troubled. He was on his ship and there were pirates again, fighting, stabbing him and carrying Nic away, over and over again. He woke at dawn to the screeching of the old red cockerel outside his window, crowing so loudly that he had no choice but to listen, and rise. He dressed quietly, and walked down to the harbour. It was getting colder these mornings, winter was not far off now. A soft white mist lay over the harbour, hugging his boat, which appeared out of that sea-cloud like an apparition. It caught at his heart to see how brown and beautiful she was, bobbing on the waves.

It was time to go. He knew that. There was no longer a reason to stay here, among these friendly people who had looked after him so well. He had to return to Athens and find Gorgias, and if he intended to compete in the Olympics, he had to fulfil the requirements—nine months of strict training. There was no more time to waste. Gellius turned back and made his way slowly up the hill towards the house. Penelope saw him as he came through the door, and she cried out when she saw his face.

'You're leaving us!'

'But I'll be back.' He tried to smile. 'After the Olympic Games, exactly as I promised. I'll sail back into the harbour with my olive wreath and we'll have the biggest party you've ever seen.' Gellius tried to make her laugh, but she threw down the cloth she had been holding and ran out of the room, crying. Later, she came back, more composed.

'After you tell the father about his son, will you look for Nicasylus?'

The idea of a search had niggled at Gellius for weeks. But it would be useless—the boy could be anywhere. 'No,' he said, 'I'll have to get ready for the Games. I've got to train or I won't be allowed to participate.'

For the second time that morning, Penelope ran out of the room.

Athens was a shambles. From Piraeus all the way to the city, there was nothing but death. Gellius had no way of knowing how many people this plague had claimed, but he could see that many thousands must have died. Shops were closed, houses stood empty; over everything was the smell of decay and the sound of grief.

In the city he hesitated. It was such an awful task he had undertaken, he was in no great hurry to carry it out. The Acropolis still looked beautiful; death had not dared to touch the temples of the gods. He would make his way up the hill to worship before he looked for Nic's house.

It was a long time since he had stood among the temples with their tall graceful columns, and their elegance made him feel shabby. The few men and women who stood before the great statue of the goddess stared at his rough seafaring clothes. Slowly he walked the length of the temple of Athena, and paused in front of the great golden statue of the goddess. The captain closed his eyes, and prayed.

Athens had been his city once. He had grown up there, before he made his way to the port of Piraeus and began to work a trading vessel along the coast. The best person to help him now was his old friend— the captain of the first boat he'd ever been on, Porinus. It was Porinus who had lent him the money to begin trading—a debt that was repaid quickly; trading came naturally to Gellius and he loved the life. Two years had passed since they'd met, but when Porinus opened the door it was as if no time had passed at all. He smiled widely and welcomed Gellius inside.

'Wine!' The older man clapped his hands and the household slave scurried off to fill the goblets.

'Has your ship been profitable, Gellius?' Porinus leaned forward a little in his seat. 'Did I train you well in the art of trading?'

'Very well.' Gellius laughed. 'I've done a roaring business, enough to pay my way to Olympia.'

'You're going at last? To compete in the Pankration? Wonderful news!' Porinus straightened up, and grimaced. 'I'm afraid my days as a Pankratiast are well and truly gone. I hurt my back last week and now I'm walking round like an old man.'

'You are an old man!'

They laughed together like children, the first time Gellius could remember laughing like that since the night on deck with Nic. The thought made him serious again. He put down his cup and stood up.

'I'm here on business,' he said quietly. His hands wouldn't stay still, he fiddled with the carved edge of the table. 'It's about a passenger I took on board my ship when the plague first began.'

Gellius told his old friend the whole story.

'I couldn't stop them from carrying him off. I tried, Porinus, but I was too badly injured. If the fishermen hadn't found me, I'd have died out there. Now I need to find the boy's family, and let them know.' A rueful smile played around his lips. 'I could never look Penelope in the eye again if I didn't.' Gellius looked serious again. 'The boy's stepfather is Gorgias, the goldsmith. Do you know him?'

'Everyone knew Gorgias,' the old man said slowly. 'His work was the best in the city; individual and detailed. I have a piece of his that I bought for my wife.' He sighed. 'The plague took him. His wife first, then he died a month ago. A terrible waste.' The old sailor shook his head.

'He mentioned his sister to me. She'd been married just before Nicasylus left the city. Do you know if she's alive still?'

'Artemis? Yes, she's still alive, but her husband isn't.

She lives with her father-in-law now. I hear the house is full of women, and the old fellow is going crazy. All his sons died and he has the care of the wives, since there's a distinct shortage of eligible men to claim them these days.' Porinus's eyes were moist, his hands shook a little as he lifted his cup to his lips. 'Between the war with Sparta and the plague, half our young men have died. All that life and talent, thrown away. Yet old men like me survived, and what do I have to offer Greece?'

'Ah, friend,' Gellius reached out and touched the other man's arm, 'you have so much. For a start, you can train me. You still know more about the Pank-ration than any man alive.'

'Nothing would make me happier.' Porinus's face had become lively; he straightened his back the tiniest fraction and then grimaced. Gellius laughed.

'Don't strain yourself, old man. Not before we've even started! I need you in top form if you're going to help me win the olive crown for Athens.' A slave came in and set a dish of fresh figs on the table along-side the men. Gellius popped one in his mouth and let the sweet juices roll over his tongue. 'Always a wonderful host, Porinus.' He indicated the fruit. 'I am afraid that poor Nic is not eating fresh figs right now, wherever he is. I must go to the boy's sister. I have to tell her what I know.' He felt more anxious about this task than he would have about fighting a hundred

69

pirates, but it couldn't be put off any longer.

'Time for that in the morning.' Porinus refilled his cup with wine. 'You can't possibly go to her at night with news like that. It's better she learns her brother's fate when there's sun to keep her fears at bay. I'll take you myself in the morning. Now, let's discuss your training.' He kneaded his hands together. 'This is the challenge I've waited for!'

They sat late into the night talking and drinking and planning the next nine months of training. There was so much to discuss that it was very late before they retired to their beds to sleep.

When the sun woke him in the morning, Gellius had to shield his eyes. His head hurt from too much wine and talk the night before. He ate a simple breakfast, and he and Porinus made their way slowly across the city.

At the house it was the girl's father-in-law who received them, and Gellius became practically speechless. His tongue was like a ball of wool in his mouth. There was no easy way to say that someone's only brother was missing, stolen by pirates somewhere off the coast of Greece. He hesitated so often that in the end it was Porinus who told the story, and when he had finished, there was a scream from somewhere nearby. A young woman burst into the room, ignoring the protestations of her father-in-law. She had ivory skin and black hair, and her face was so wild and full

70

of pain and fear that Gellius stepped backwards invol-
untarily. She faced him, passionately begging him to
say it wasn't true.

'I'm sorry,' he stammered. 'I'm sorry.'

Gellius caught her as she fell.

CHAPTER

8

Nic fitted a large stone to his slingshot, where it nestled snugly against the soft leather pouch. He gripped the surface of that huge granite boulder and clambered up it, guided by the bleating of the little goat. That sound was a good sign. It meant the wolf hadn't yet reached its prey. He climbed on and on, his breathing heavy, as if he were blowing air through water. He was struggling up a steep part of the mountain, and adrenalin was all that kept him moving now; that and the urge to rescue his animal.

As Nic cleared a rise, he saw the wolf, loping across relatively flat land. Directly in its path, fixed to the ground like something that had been stitched to the landscape, was his goat. Its bleating rose to a sharp crescendo and stopped mid-note as the wolf swept the small body off the ground and shook it the way a cat might shake a rat. Nic's scream took over where his goat's had stopped. He began to spin the long, thin straps of his slingshot, in a lazy, curling ring that exploded with swift acceleration. The stone struck the wolf between the eyes. It hit the ground, a landslide of heavy flesh, and the kid, not yet dead, rolled out of its jaws. Nic darted forward instinctively and took it gently into his arms—and in the same moment a terrible weight thumped at his back. His knees buckled. Hands wet and sticky with blood, Nic felt the little goat slide from his fingers as if greased.

The wolf was trying to roll him over. Nic grabbed a rock and bashed it across the side of the wolf's head with all the strength he had left. The animal made a sound that was almost human, a low, savage groan, and retreated. There was no time to think, Nic got to his feet and ran full tilt across the open ground. The goat came into view unexpectedly on the rock ahead of him. A slick of blood trailed down the granite and was pooling on the ground beneath. Nic stared at what lay beyond, understanding why the kid had stopped. Before them both the land fell away into a deep crevasse.

Nic turned to face the wolf. He felt unexpectedly calm all of a sudden, as if everything were perfectly normal. He had time to watch the wolf's face as it loped slowly towards him and time to realise its intention. It didn't want him. It lunged at the kid, making it fly out into the night sky like a limp white doll. The dark body of the wolf followed in a clumsy arc.

Afterwards Nic could only remember two things. The wolf's eyes, formidable and yet with a look of detachment as if it knew it was already dead, and its underbelly. It was pregnant.

It took longer to get back down to the hut than it had done to climb up in the first place. Nic stumbled and slid, scraping most of the skin off his legs and knees and arms and hands. He was crying and the salty tears stung wherever they fell. He had to force himself the last little way; the open wounds on his back and shoulder were making his muscles lock. It was an enormous relief to see the hut loom into view, and he collapsed onto his straw pallet the moment he stumbled inside.

It was like dreaming while being totally awake. Everything seemed to be etched into his brain—he wished the visions would go away, and he wished he had something warm to wrap himself in; the night had suddenly become freezing cold. He forced himself to think. The wounds on his back were aching and bloody. Strips of cloth torn from his tunic made a reasonable bandage, but it was difficult and painful to tie around his chest. Nic packed the wound with clean straw from his bed and lay back, exhausted from the effort it had taken. There was no point in trying to negotiate the mountain in the dark. He would have

74

to wait till morning. He turned his body to the wall of the hut and closed his eyes.

The loss of another goat, his torn tunic, lacerations to his body that required a week away from his herd to mend and another two weeks on light, household duties after that—all these earned him the anger of his master when he got back; but at least he wasn't beaten this time. Among the slaves a grudging respect emerged—to defeat a wild animal in such circumstances was unheard of. He was asked to tell the story over and over again in all its gory details. Only Scopas refused to speak to Nic and whenever the story was repeated by anyone, he would butt in nastily. 'It's all a lie. Did anyone actually see this wolf? No. It conveniently slipped off the mountain and disappeared. He could have got those cuts falling down the mountainside himself; he's clumsy enough. I for one have never seen that little runt do a single thing that was brave or strong. I bet he made the whole thing up.'

They were all asleep. Nic was dreaming about Artemis, seeing her running towards him with her arms open wide and a look of joy on her face. She was crying and laughing and then, without warning, he was awake, choking. Scopas had his arm around Nic's neck, pulling tight.

'You lying little thief!' he hissed in Nic's ear. 'You

75

might have tricked all the others with your made-up stories, your pretence of being a hero, but you haven't fooled me. You've stolen my new slingshot, haven't you?'

He pushed Nic in the back with a hard knee. The knuckles of his left hand punched brutally into Nic's side.

'I ought to kill you, nobody will ever miss you. Let's see how strong you are against another man this time. Maybe a wolf's too easy for a boy like you, eh?'

'I haven't got your slingshot, I swear! The one I carry is the one I made myself.' Nic could barely speak, his eyes were bulging from the pressure on his neck, and his voice came out as a squeak.

'I don't believe you, runt. You tell lies too easily. Where's your superhuman strength now when you need it? Eh?' All the time he was whispering and tightening his grip around Nic's throat with his elbow. At any moment, Nic was going to pass out; he could feel the blood singing in his ears. Then, abruptly, the arm released its hold. Scopas fell on top of him, a dead weight. When Nic rolled out from underneath, he saw why. Sticking out of the slave's back was a short dagger and standing over him was Tiso.

'What have you done?' Nic whispered. 'He's dead, you've killed him.' There would be a savage punishment for the loss of the slave. Scopas was big and strong and well-trained, he was valuable. 'You'll be put to death for this, Tiso, what were you thinking?'

Tiso stood dumb. He simply pointed to Scopas's body. In the slave's right hand, tightly clasped in the fingers still, was a short-handled knife. Tiso pulled a finger across his own throat in an unmistakable gesture. Scopas had intended to kill him! Nic stood staring at the blade, unable to take it in.

Tiso pulled a face and indicated the door with a jerk of his head. 'Time to get going,' he was clearly saying. Nic hesitated. A runaway slave could be seized and beaten senseless; the punishment, if he were caught, would be at best almost unendurable. At worst, it was death. Tiso bent down and prised open Scopas's fingers, letting the knife fall with a clatter. He retrieved his own dagger and wiped it clean on the dead boy's tunic, then calmly walked to the door and opened it. He clapped his huge hands around Scopas's ankles and dragged him across the floor, through the door and into the bushes outside. He soaked up the blood by spreading fresh sand across the floor, then sweeping it up, and it was all done silently, as though it was no more than any of the usual household duties.

The evening was warm, the moon was full in the sky and its light showed clearly every detail of build-ings, trees and rocks and the path that led down the hill. Tiso indicated that he was finished and began to walk away. Nic followed silently, afraid for his life now in a way he had never been before, not even on the deck of the pirate ship. But what he was doing, he realised with sudden clarity, was inevitable. Sooner or later, he would have had to run away. Now he had no choice—Scopas had made sure of that. His heart jumped at the thought of the other boy, dead. There was such a small moment between life and death.

They began their journey like two ordinary people going for an evening stroll. Anyone observing them would have seen no sign of haste or panic, just a man and a boy walking casually towards the harbour. It was not until they were out of sight of the house and the farm was far behind them that they began to run. Tiso set the pace, sprinting with a swiftness that Nic could barely match, but the effort made the older man shake and brought the sweat pouring from his black skin. As soon as they stopped he doubled over with the worst coughing fit Nic had ever heard. Breathless and with aching muscles they cast about for some way of escaping further. A stone wall ringed the harbour, and from it a narrow dock jutted out into the water. A small fishing boat, silver in the moonlight, was bobbing on the gentle swell, tied to the pier by a short length of rope. Tiso reached down and undid it, signalling that Nic should climb aboard. He didn't hesitate. It was a night like the one when he had left Piraeus. A picture of Gellius's face rose up in his mind and it was a comfort to him. He just prayed that this time, there would be no pirates afloat.

They rowed out into the bay with strong, even strokes, and the ebbing tide helped to carry the little craft well beyond the headlands. In a very short time, they were at sea.

CHAPTER
9

Keeping in as near to the shore as they dared, Nic and Tiso took turns to row. Sometimes their muscles went into spasm and their backs felt so stiff they were literally in agony, but still they rowed on doggedly. Nothing could be worse than capture; they must put as much distance as possible between themselves and the farm before morning, when Scopas's body would be found.

It was dawn when Tiso signalled a stop. The sea was calm and they were moving parallel to a rocky piece of shoreline which seemed to offer no anchorage or harbour. He waited until they were so close to the shore they could almost have reached out and touched anyone standing there before he leapt into the water and began to drag the boat the last few metres. Nic joined him and together they lifted the boat, carried it over the rocks to a small group of low trees, upturned it and piled shrubbery on top. No other craft were visible, and there were certainly no moorings suggesting that any might come later. It seemed perfect. Tiso indicated that Nic should rest. He mimed walking, then eating food. He must have been as exhausted as Nic, who was utterly worn out by the rowing, but he clearly intended to find food before he rested.

When Nic woke, the sun was well down in the west. Tiso was asleep alongside him with a mound of food—figs and olives and bread—in a small pile near his head. Nic ate a little. He had long since learned not to wolf his food down, but to eat it in small bites which he chewed slowly; his days on the mountain with the goats had taught him that. When he had satisfied his body's urgent need for food, he felt able to look about him. There was no sign of habitation, but the bread was fresh and the olives had been well cured. Nic wondered how far they had come, and where exactly they were. There was no way of telling. All he knew was that they were a long way from Athens, and had little chance of ever making it back there in one piece. If they were not caught as runaway slaves, they ran the risk of being caught stealing food.

Tiso coughed and sat up as the sun dipped below the horizon. He yawned, smiled and began to chew some of the bread in a comical rolling fashion, the way a bird might manage a lump of bread that was too big

The rim sank slowly, surrounding the silvery fish with a soft balloon of fine netting and dropping to the sand beneath as the weights dragged it down like a bag. They got more than they could possibly eat. Unlike Nic, who could barely swallow one of the slimy, scaly creatures, Tiso seemed to savour the raw fish, eating more than a dozen before he fell asleep in the shade of rocks near the water's edge. The next night, after they had set out again, he showed Nic how to troll behind the boat with a little spinning line he had baited with a piece of sardine flesh. Towards morning they caught a large fish. It thrashed about in the bottom of the boat, scales flashing in the moonlight until Tiso smacked its head sharply on the gunwale. Tiso's resourcefulness amazed Nic. Next morning he somehow conjured sparks from a piece of flint and dry seaweed. Cooked over a fire on the beach the fish was the most delicious thing Nic had ever tasted. He thought of all the times at home in Athens when fish had been served and he had turned up his nose at the cook's offering. He really thought he could eat almost anything now.

Despite their predicament, they found themselves laughing a lot, enjoying each other's company and their extraordinary freedom. So far they had not discussed where they were going, they were merely getting as far away from the farm as possible. Nic himself hoped to get back to Greece and then to

Athens, but he doubted that Tiso even knew where Greece was. It seemed he had come from Constantinople on a slave-trader. Nic had managed to work that out from what little he was able to understand of his companion's guttural sounds and elaborate mimes.

He was an amazingly strong man—he could row for hours and often did. The only things that stopped him or slowed him down were the coughing fits that frequently racked his body. Afterwards he would take a while to recover his breath, but still, he made good time in the little boat whenever it was his turn to row.

Nic was not able to decide whether they were heading in the right direction because he didn't know exactly where they had come from; but one thing in his favour was that he knew the stars in the heavens so well. He just had to get them back overhead in the right pattern, and they could work out a course to Greece.

Every day as he slept, and all through each monotonously tiring night, thoughts of his mother and Gorgias, of Artemis, and of Gellius, that brave sea captain, rolled around in his mind like a tangle of string. How many of them were left alive? Would he ever see them again?

He wished with all his heart that he knew how to reach his country. Poseidon, the great god of the sea, seemed happy to provide them with fish and octopus each day. Perhaps he would also lead Nic back across the water to home.

CHAPTER

10

Gellius put all his energies into the training pro-
gramme that Porinus worked out for him. He stuck
to a special diet; walked, ran and daily threw himself
at the heavy bag of grain that hung from the gymnasium roof until he thought he'd drop from exhaustion.
Often his mind turned to Artemis. That she loved her
brother was obvious, that her own life was miserable
was even plainer. Clearly her father-in-law's household was under considerable strain. All the extra wives
made the place crowded and uncomfortable, yet
custom dictated that women be given a home until a
suitable marriage could be made; not an easy thing to
do since so many men had died. Gellius did what he
could, leaving small gifts of food and clothing.
Occasionally he saw Artemis drawing water from the
fountain, but it was not permitted to speak to her

there. She would look up and flash a shy smile before hurrying on with the heavy amphora of water on her head. Once they passed in the street and she timidly acknowledged his greeting with a small nod of her pretty head, then went swiftly on her way.

'Put it all behind you, Gellius,' advised Porinus. 'Time to get on with the training for your event. There's nothing more you can do about the boy, anyway.'

He was right, and Gellius knew it. Still he couldn't help but think about Nic, and wonder what had become of him. As for Artemis, he had to admit it wasn't just guilt about her brother that made him think of her so often. He might have said, if anyone had asked, that he was falling in love.

The gymnasium was the only place where he ever managed to forget both Artemis and her brother for more than a few minutes. Porinus had found him a wonderful sparring partner: a wrestler named Phrixus who had once won the olive crown for Athens. Phrixus was pleased to have a man to spar with, especially a man of Gellius's strength. Each day they began with the ritual cleansing, bathing and anointing their bodies with oil. In the dust room they threw sand and dust at each other to roughen their bodies and provide a firmer grasp. Gellius practised all the holds, as Phrixus showed him ways of twisting and turning his body beneath the steely grasp of an opponent.

'It's an old saying, friend.' Phrixus stopped a moment to catch his breath between rounds. 'A Pankratiast must have the strength of a lion and the cunning of a fox. So far you have the smell of a fox and the laziness of a lion with a full belly.' He spun lightly away as Gellius roared and threw himself forwards. 'Don't let your temper drive you,' he chided as Gellius toppled past. 'Anger always has a bad aim.'

From the sidelines, Porinus laughed.

'Better listen, Gellius. You've always been too hot-tempered. If you're going to win the Pankration, you need to learn to be calm. You need to sense the exact moment to let your opponent feel he can slip away, *then* apply the hold that will cripple him. It's all a question of timing, strength and level-headedness. You've already got the strength. Now you need to develop a strategy for the other things.'

Gellius took it all in his stride. He was too good-natured to ever complain or be really bad-tempered. He just started again, head down, his whole body tensed for the next encounter.

When Porinus tied a dead sheep to the rafters in the gymnasium, Gellius laughed.

'Surely you don't expect me to fight a dead animal?' he asked. 'What can I learn from that?'

'How to dislocate its feet, how to gouge its eyes!' Porinus was serious. 'You'd better learn to fight dirty,

87

Gellius. Your opponents may not all be gentlemen like you.'

'I'll leave that kind of fighting to men who can do those things with a clear conscience—I can't.' The captain shrugged his massive shoulders. 'I'll win because I deserve to win.'

'You're a fool, Gellius. A Pankratiast must inflict pain, it's the only way to win a match.'

'Inflict pain, yes. I'll do everything within my power to make my opponent suffer, but I won't maim him or leave him blinded. That isn't sport, it's war.'

Porinus cut down the sheep.

For nine months the three men worked together. Gellius never left the ring without bruises and often blood on his body somewhere. His hands became so strong that if he stretched the fingers of one hand out flat, nobody was able to bend as much as the little finger.

'If you don't have strong fingers you can kiss the olive wreath goodbye,' Porinus often said. He and Phrixus had both encountered contestants in the Pankration who loved to dislocate their opponent's fingers. 'You have to think of them as iron bars, Gellius, not flesh and blood.'

By the time he left the gymnasium each day, Gellius could have eaten a horse. It was customary to train on an empty stomach, and when he did eat it was a vegetarian diet he followed; barley bread, wheat porridge, fruit and nuts and a little cheese. He was constantly hungry. Porinus, however, delighted in bringing for himself cooked meat or a jug of wine which he ate and drank with relish. One day Gellius could stand it no longer

'Porinus,' he cried in frustration, 'can't you see how it upsets me to watch you eat that meat?'

'Get used to it, Gellius.' Porinus smacked his lips and took another huge bite. 'If just the sight of food is enough to unsettle you, then any opponent is going to have an easy time with you. You have to get *all* your feelings in check, to win the Pankration. You can't afford to have one loose emotion or it'll leap out and strangle you.'

Gellius began to sleep on the ground, on the skin of a steer. At Olympia this would be his bed and he needed to be ready. Now he doubled his exercise routines and increased the ferocity of the sparring matches until Porinus had to call for him to slow down.

'Phrixus will be no good to you dead, Gellius. Go easy on the poor man!'

Just before they were to set out for Elis and the training camp, he saw Artemis. She was on her way to the fountain house, and she looked particularly beautiful. Gellius took his courage in both hands and stepped into her path. He'd never have spoken to a married woman like this usually, but now was no time to observe the social niceties.

'I'm leaving for Olympia soon.' He faltered. 'I told your brother I'd go this year and that I'd take him with me.' Artemis stared, not a word passed her lips. 'I know it's ridiculous, but I keep thinking that if it's in any way possible, Nic will make his way to Olympia too. We said that we'd be there this year, you see.' The words began to dry up on his tongue. Artemis was staring at him with those beautiful brown eyes of hers, her lip was trembling and he was afraid that she might suddenly burst into tears.

'I'll be searching for him,' he finished weakly. 'If I can, I'll find him.'

'I'll pray for you.' Her voice was soft and faint. 'That you will win your event'—she blushed as she said that—'and that the gods will be kind to us all, and return Nicasylus to me.' She turned swiftly and was gone before he could reply.

Gellius drifted off like a love-struck boy. He felt as if he could have won a hundred bouts, against the fiercest fighters anywhere in Greece. How he hoped and prayed that he could return from Olympia with the two prizes he desired above all others: the olive crown, and the boy, Nicasylus.

chapter 11

'Back here, Tiso! Quickly, before they see us.' Nic shoved at the baskets stacked on the grimy wharf and managed to open up a space big enough for them to crawl into. With some difficulty the big man pushed through and Nic wriggled in behind him, pulling a sack down on top to close the gap. With luck they'd be hidden from the two men he'd just seen coming down the wharf. The afternoon shadows cast long fingers among the baskets and barrels around them, enough to keep them hidden if Tiso's cough didn't betray them. It had grown steadily worse lately and slowed him down so much that it had taken the whole day to cover a very short distance.

'Be still.' Nic's voice was a whisper. 'Just be perfectly quiet and they'll go past.'

Tiso looked sick. Over the past few weeks the poor

wretch had been hacking and spluttering constantly. Nic had seen blood in his spittle. He'd grown slower and wearier, and since yesterday a raging fever had racked his tired body, making him tremble and shake constantly. It was obviously a tremendous effort for him to keep going. They'd been forced to abandon the fishing boat many weeks back because the rugged coastline offered no anchorage, and there'd been no villages where they could get food. Since then they had been making their way slowly across the country-side—through groves of wild cypress and tall scrubby trees for the past few days—before reaching this port. It was so beautiful, so like home, that Nic was almost fooled into believing they were getting close. But then the sun had come out from behind the clouds and he knew they were nowhere near home, for if this had been Greece, the landscape would have been translu-cent with the liquid gold light that all Greeks loved.

Nic had managed to steal a skin of wine and some bread, but little else for the entire day. The wharf, with its stacks of bales and baskets, had seemed as good a place as any to scrounge some food. It surprised him how easily he had adapted to stealing. His father would turn in his grave—but then perhaps not: he would have wanted Nic to stay alive.

Tiso had begun to shiver, with ferocious vibrations that made his teeth chatter and his limbs twitch invol-untarily. He tried to control the shaking by wrapping his arms around his knees, but the silent shuddering went on uninterrupted. Outside the sound of voices was uncomfortably close; Nic concentrated on staying calm and quiet. A faint smell, like dried fish, was seeping out of the dusty baskets that surrounded them—it was the smell that had attracted him to the spot in the first place. He could have gnawed his way through the cane, he was so hungry; instead he sucked a little wine from the goatskin pouch and tried to settle himself. There was no room to move with Tiso slumped against his back; it was dusty and airless and his legs were beginning to cramp. The desire to stretch them grew greater every moment.

Nic held his breath, trying to stifle the sneeze that was working its way up his nose like a lit fuse, because suddenly, he could plainly hear what the voices were saying.

'Port officials say they were seen around here this morning,' said one. 'The lad on his own would be hard to pick, but since he's with the black man, we shouldn't have too much trouble.'

Next moment other men, calling out to each other in a language Nic didn't understand, interrupted the searchers, and their heavy footsteps retreated. Nic breathed more easily, but it was obvious that if they stayed where they were, they ran the risk of being discovered as the ship was loaded.

'Tiso,' Nic whispered, 'we should climb aboard this

ship, now. Wherever she's going, it has to be better than staying here.' He didn't like the idea very much, but he couldn't think of anything else. These men sounded like professionals, well paid to find absconding slaves and trained for the job. Unless he and Tiso managed to discover somewhere better to hide, their fate was certain.

By now Tiso couldn't even manage a nod. His face was ghostly pale and his skin temperature alternated between raging heat and shuddering cold. His big body was curled into a ball, knees against chest with his head lolled over like a dead weight. It was frightening to see him like this. Cautiously Nic pushed the sack away and peered over the top of the baskets. He could see the men walking slowly along the wharf, looking around them as they went. The leisurely manner in which they went about their business sent a cold shiver up Nic's back.

Activity on the dock was slowing down. Slaves were still loading heavy bales and bundles, but they lingered over each task as if they were just waiting for the signal to stop work. Not far away two men were deep in conversation about winds, the weather and the prices being fetched for silver and cloth. They had their backs turned to Nic, but he felt his heart pounding in his chest as he contemplated the enormous risk entailed in sliding out from that hiding place and trying to board the ship without being seen. Still, what choice did they have?

'Tiso,' he prodded his friend gently with his foot. 'We must plan!' There was no reply. Nic bent down and shook him, but the slave had fallen asleep where he sat, and no amount of whispered persuasion, shaking or prodding could rouse him.

Nic sneaked another look around the dock. The slaves were being marshalled into groups—some were already moving off. As soon as the sun had set, they could attempt to climb aboard the ship under cover of darkness.

'Sleep on, Tiso. We've got a little while to wait.' He bent down. Tiso's breathing was more laboured; it rose and fell raggedly and there was a sheen on his black skin, as though a wet film had settled all over him. Nic felt his forehead and was astonished at how hot it was. He had a severe fever, that was for certain; water was what he needed but there was only the wine. Nic dabbed some onto Tiso's dry, peeling lips. He couldn't do anything more for him. Until the sun went down at least, they must stay where they were.

Tiso's breathing was so loud and rasping that Nic had to cover his mouth when people came anywhere near. Nic became more and more anxious. It seemed to take forever before the activity on the dock ceased altogether, and all the while, Tiso became sicker. Nic was frantic. How could he ever manage to get Tiso up and drag him across the dock and onto the boat?—he was clearly incapable of getting himself on board. In fact, by now he was hallucinating, muttering and moaning. There was no way of getting him onto the boat, and no way he could be left. Nic stayed where he was, huddled next to Tiso's body, which burned like a slow fire that grew weaker and weaker as the night wore on.

Before dawn, as a stiff breeze from over the water cut a chilly swathe through the basket barricade that enclosed them, Tiso began to take longer, heaving breaths, the air in his lungs rattling and gurgling like water knocking about inside a pipe. There was a kind of rhythm to the cycle; a shallow breath, then silence for so long it seemed that must have been the last—but no, another breath, long and raucous this time, sustained the racked body for a few more moments. Nic cradled Tiso's head in his arms and waited. He realised that it was only a matter of time now. His friend would not be completing the journey to Greece—Tiso's journey was to be of another sort altogether.

Stroking the big man's head gently, Nic hummed a simple tune he remembered from when Artemis had played her flute, on nights just like this one—dark and cold and lonely. Memories of Tiso filled his mind: the times the black slave had stopped the mindless, cruel torment that Scopas had enjoyed so much; the many times Tiso had slipped a little extra food into Nic's pouch—and the cough that had been his trademark sound. Maybe Tiso had known this illness would kill him before much longer. He'd had nothing left to lose when he killed Scopas. Nic let himself cry, and cry and cry.

In the pale, grey hour before dawn, as the tide ebbed and the moon faded, Tiso took one last rattling, gurgling breath. It was the last living sound he made. He died. It was as simple as that. Nic laid his friend's head back against the baskets. Letting go wasn't so easy. Nic touched his fingers on Tiso's cheek, and drew the eyelids down over the open, staring eyes.

'Goodbye, friend.' His voice was a whisper.

There was no way of performing the rites, nor of carrying out any burial. Nic made do with saying his own prayers over Tiso's body. At last he looked cautiously over the top of the baskets. Dawn was lighting the eastern sky; no one was moving about yet. Without a backwards look, Nic ran swiftly across the dock and clambered silently aboard the ship. Its creaking timbers and the exotic smells of the cargo were so oddly familiar, he felt instantly comfortable. Creeping into a dark space deep in the hold, he curled up snugly, the wineskin close to his chest. He needed sleep. Just the way he had felt when he boarded Gellius's boat, the boy thought drowsily.

When he woke again, he could feel the freighter was well under way. The only question left in his oddly empty mind, was, where was it headed?

CHAPTER

12

In the centre of the agora, the *Spondophoros* took up his position. Throughout the marketplace, men stopped what they were doing to listen. He was a herald, travelling the length and breadth of Greece to announce the Olympic Games.

'Any free-born Greek'—the man lifted his voice a fraction, staring down on the agora sternly—'who has committed no deed of violence and has not incurred the wrath of the gods, may take part in the Games.' He paused. The indications were that the contingent from Athens would not be very large this year. The plague had taken so many young men; and besides, since then, all sense of right and wrong seemed to have deserted the people of Athens. The old, sacred ways of burial had been abandoned—people tossed their lifeless relatives and friends on top of other people's funeral pyres and went off as quickly as possible. And it had become normal to see men looting a dead person's house or business; there was no reason to care about anybody else when in a week or so you could be dead.

'And may the world be free of murder and crime and the rattle of weapons silenced.' In his measured and quiet way, the *Spondophoros* climbed back down from his podium. He had proclaimed the Sacred Truce, now he must move on to other cities and towns to do the same. Three heralds were out on the roads now, declaring the truce throughout Greece so that all who wished could travel in safety to the Games. By the first full moon of midsummer, thousands of men would arrive at the sacred Altis in Olympia to celebrate the eighty-eighth Games.

From their position next to the Altar of the Twelve Gods, Gellius and Porinus watched the herald with great interest.

'Well, Gellius,' Porinus smoothed his chiton with one thin hand and began to walk away, 'it's time to leave. If we're going to get to Elis in time, we must be on our way. It's a long journey to Olympia.'

The old Pankratiast stumbled a little and almost fell. Gellius had to reach out and grab his arm to steady him.

'Are you all right?' Gellius was concerned.

'Just tired, that's all. Once we're on our way to

99

Olympia, I'll feel better.' Porinus ran his fingers through the thin strands of silvery hair that barely covered his head. He was looking old, Gellius realised. 'This place depresses me. War and plague and lawlessness. I'll be glad to get out for a while.'

Gellius nodded. 'It's so different now. I never thought I'd be glad to leave Athens, but I will be.' He walked silently beside Porinus as they made their way back through the city. Maybe the trip to Olympia would restore the balance, make him feel once again what it was to be Athenian, competing for the honour of the city he loved.

That night he packed. Nothing much; he owned only two pairs of sandals, one of which he wore, another chiton, and a pouch that contained his money. Food he'd be able to buy along the way from the hundreds of food sellers who always thronged the road to Olympia. Whatever he needed there'd be someone eager to sell it to him. Just the thought of the trip was wonderful: the music and jugglers and storytellers, the animals being taken for sacrifice, and all the colour and excitement of ordinary and extraordinary people heading to the Games. Gellius was ready for this trip, he'd been getting ready all his life. Just to compete at Olympia was an honour he looked forward to eagerly. He refused to allow himself to think about who his opponents might be. Somewhere else in Greece they were

100

getting ready right now, and they hoped, just as much as he did, to be victorious.

Even before dawn broke, the road out of Athens was crowded with travellers bound for the Games. Porinus and Gellius had set off a little later than most, a concession to Porinus's age. He disliked early mornings and preferred to stay in bed as long as he could.

'You're getting soft in your old age, Porinus,' Gellius chided him. 'Used to be a time when you could have run the first fifty *stade*, naked, before dawn. Look at you now, creeping along on a donkey.'

'Even the best Pankratiast grows old.' The trainer's eyes stared into the distance. 'It comes to us all. Anyway, where's your victory statue, Gellius?' Porinus was laughing. 'You have commissioned it, haven't you?'

'When I set out for the next Games, old man,' Gellius retorted. 'That'll give me time to get a really good statue made, instead of a rushed job.'

They both laughed. The morning was clear and crisp—a fresh rain had settled the dust. As they made their way out of Athens, mounted on the two good mules Porinus had bought for the trip, they joked like schoolboys and everything they saw made them smile. It felt so good to leave.

The fields and the mountains and even the sea were

all brushed with the honey-gold, transparent light Gellius loved. Morning sun in Greece, filtered through a sky the blue of the Aegean—this was the colour of Greece's soul, he thought. If she could ever stop fighting herself. For now, anyway, there would be three months of peace while all over the country athletes, kings, philosophers and statesmen set out for the Games. The five roads to Olympia would all be filled with wonderful processions of men and beasts and gifts for the gods. Gellius had brought his father's helmet— engraved with his name and birth and glorious death in battle. It would be an honour to leave it in the sacred *Altis* for Zeus.

The mules clattered along slowly, the two men at times silent and watchful, sometimes noisy and laughing. It was an adventure Gellius wouldn't have missed for the world. Everything he'd done for five long years had been for this.

He was on his way to Olympia as a Pankratiast, at last.

CHAPTER

13

Nic woke to the soothing sound of oars slapping against the water. It was hot and airless in the hull with a mixture of salt and sour smells that made him suddenly think of fresh water. Thirst choked his throat like dust, he could hardly swallow he was so desperate to drink. He climbed the narrow ladder to the deck in a sweat of fear and thirst.

'I wondered when you'd come up.'

Nic's head swivelled in the direction of the voice. At the bow stood a man Nic took to be the captain, and he was speaking perfect Athenian Greek.

'And who are you, boy?' There was something belligerent and yet hesitant about the captain's voice. His wild black eyebrows were beetling at Nic in such a fierce way that Nic trembled; but nothing could divert him from getting a drink.

'Nicasylus of the house of Gorgias, goldsmith of Athens; I need water.'

The captain laughed. 'There's water behind you in a jug. Help yourself.'

Nic drank from the jug directly, swallowing silently; as if his gullet had simply opened up like a pipe. When he stopped he could hear the water slopping round in his stomach.

'So, son of Gorgias, why are you wearing clothes fit only for a beggar and hiding in my stinking cargo hold?' The captain's eyebrows twisted themselves into fat caterpillars that practically crawled off his face. It was beginning to make Nic smile. 'Start at the beginning.'

It took him an hour to tell the whole story. Even then he had to leave out a lot.

'I'm going home,' he finished, 'I want to see Artemis and Mother and Gorgias again.'

The captain kept his mouth shut. To his certain knowledge, the goldsmith was dead of plague—he'd tried to buy one of the craftsman's rings last time he was in Athens. Quite likely the rest of the family was dead as well. The house had been boarded up. Still, the kid would find out soon enough.

'I keep wondering about Gellius. If he survived or not.' Nicasylus stared out to sea. 'I think if he did, he'd go to Olympia for the Games. We arranged to go together this year—he was going to compete in the Pankration.'

'Well, you've landed on your feet, boy. You've picked a Greek ship sailing from Syracuse to Patras. We'll be there in a day, and from there it's not far to Olympia. You'll have all the company you'd ever need on the road, too. The port will be literally swarming with men on their way to the Games. You couldn't have got a more direct path if you'd asked the gods for a map.'

It was better than Nic could possibly have imagined.

'We sail back to Corcyra after that. Too far away to help you get to Athens, but you should have no difficulty getting home. The Sacred Truce will see you safely there, and there'll be plenty of good men on the road. Your stepfather was a well-respected man. You need only mention his name and you'll find help, I'm sure, even if you don't meet up with your friend, the brave sea captain.'

Privately he thought that if only half of what the lad said about the pirates was true there wasn't a hope the Pankratiast would be competing. He was more likely to have joined all the other dead men at the bottom of the Aegean. Still the captain wasn't a man to dash anyone's hopes. He fed the lad, and let Nic talk until finally he fell asleep, curled up on the wooden decking as if it were a soft bed. The captain watched Nic from his position on the bow. Perhaps the boy had the gods on his side. Perhaps his journey was protected by them—he'd certainly had a lucky run up till now.

As Nic slept, the ship ploughed on under sail, a lone oarsman at the stern. The bright blue eye on her prow guarded them all as the boat cut a swathe through the water, and the timbers squealed with the strain.

When Nic woke, it was evening. The sky above looked suddenly more familiar; they were closer to home. He could smell it in the air. Nicasylus walked across the deck and leaned over the rail, looking down into the black water that skimmed away beneath them.

'No falling in, boy.' The captain appeared at his elbow. 'I don't want to have to fish you out of the sea. Not when you've managed to get this far.' He laughed and Nic joined in. 'I was watching you sleeping. You thrashed about like a man possessed, muttering and mumbling in your dreams. I wondered what they were, you seemed so agitated.'

Nic stared at the sea, mesmerised by its black reflective surface. He had been having the same dream for weeks now.

'I was in a beautiful grove of olive trees, with great temples and statues everywhere.' His voice was just above a whisper, and the captain had to bend his head to catch all the words. 'There was an important ceremony happening around me. I heard a voice calling my name, and it said to me, "Go forward, Nicasylus. Tell the truth." But I knew that to go forward would mean my death. "Look for gold," the voice said to me. "Gold will save you." '

The captain listened gravely. He had heard the oracles speak of dreams like this one. The boy's dream was a portent of some kind, that much was clear; but what did it mean?

'Dreams like that are full of signs and symbols that take time to be revealed,' he said to the boy. 'My advice is lay it by in your mind somewhere, and when the time's right, you'll know.'

Nic nodded. He wished he felt less anxious about it. The dream seemed to be a warning, and yet he had no idea what he was being warned about. For the rest of the night he stood watch as the ship skimmed the black ocean, and he thought of Artemis. Some part of him knew, with absolute conviction, that his sister was alive. And that she expected him. And he knew there was one last great hurdle to cross, before he saw her again, even though he had no idea what that was.

Nic wrapped the light cloak around his shoulders. This time tomorrow, he would be in Olympia. The gods had brought him this far—surely they wouldn't leave him now?

The dock was a churning mass of men and animals. The noise was incredible—Nic had to shout to make himself heard.

'Where should I go? Which way is Olympia?'

'Follow the crowd, lad. You can't go wrong from here.' The captain's eyebrows met in a great bushy wedge. 'You'll need something for food. It's free otherwise. This should be enough.' He shook Nic by the hand and at the same time handed him a small pouch, ignoring Nic's protestations. 'Consider yourself helped by a fellow son of Athens. It's little enough anyway.' With a crooked smile and a wave, he turned away and Nic was left standing in the middle of the busiest port he had ever seen. It was small, compared to Piraeus, but the extra traffic caused by the Games had made it unbelievably crowded. People jostled and shouted and shoved and cursed and laughed good-naturedly. The dust and the heat were stifling. It was all Nic could do to make his way to the main road. He walked slowly along behind mules carrying heavy loads of devotional offerings and the teams of sacrificial animals who were being dragged to their deaths at Olympia. A troop of travelling players entertained everyone with impromptu play-acting, and circus artists ran alongside with fiery batons that they threw high into the air and caught again. He had never seen anything like it.

'Late in the month to be getting there, you know.' The man alongside him was speaking. 'The best camp-sites are all going to be taken, there'll just be the dregs left down near the river Alpheus. There's not a breeze to be had down in that bog, and the mosquitoes are

108

so big they can pick a man up and fly away with him!'
He laughed loudly at his own joke. 'I hope someone's
done something about getting in enough decent water
to last the week. I was so sick from the water last time,
I thought I was going to die.'

He didn't seem to need any answer from Nic, who
walked along in silence, embarrassed suddenly by his
own dirty appearance. He hadn't thought about the
way he looked for a long time. Now he wished he
could wash and change his clothes. Maybe there'd be
enough in the captain's purse to buy another chiton
from one of the clothes sellers who thronged the road.

'Did you hear what I said?'

Nic started. 'I'm sorry,' he said. 'What was it?'

'I thought you and I might hook up together this
week. You look like you could be useful to my business, and maybe I could give you a hand with what
you came here to do. Eh?'

Nic was completely perplexed. He had no idea
what the man was talking about.

'Now see that fellow up ahead?' The man slid his
arm into Nic's in a conspiratorial manner. 'An easy
mark. I'll keep him occupied while you slip his purse
out of that saddlebag on the mule. Meet me up ahead
by the grove, we'll split the purse, half each. That's
fair enough, isn't it?'

'No!' Nic was so startled he pulled his arm away
and shouted louder than he intended.

'All right. Keep your hair on.' The man seemed not to be offended. 'I was just suggesting half was fair. You keep a little extra then. I don't mind. But I think in general terms if I find the mark, then I deserve at least half.' He gave Nic a sideways smile. 'I like your spirit, boy.'

'You don't understand,' Nic began. 'I'm not ...' He got no further, a steer had broken loose and was running back down the road towards them. People were scattering in every direction and Nic had to jump for safety into the nearest ditch. By the time he climbed out again, his companion was invisible, swallowed up by the ever-growing crowd. It was a relief, really, not having to explain to the man that he wasn't a thief, just an ordinary boy who, with the goddess Athena's help, was going to Olympia for the Games.

Now he only hoped that the goddess would continue her good work. He prayed that Gellius would be in Olympia as well.

CHAPTER

14

The hill of Cronos was alive with people. If he stared too long at the sight, Nic's eyes began to play tricks and the campsites and people merged and moved like a living sea.

'Fresh honey cakes!' 'Smoked fish!' 'Lovely fresh bread!' The food-sellers were shouting over each other in a noisy attempt to lure in customers. An extraordinary mix of smells wafting across the crowded spaces did an even better job of convincing people to buy.

Nic examined his purse. The captain had been more than generous; there was a lot of money left still, but he'd have to be careful. It might have to last all the way to Athens if he couldn't find Gellius. As he elbowed his way through the crowd to the booths he could see just behind them a beautiful grove of olive trees and the newly built temple of Zeus. The richest of the tents were clustered nearby, gorgeous things that hung like butterfly wings in the still air. Wealthy men moved among them, chatting. Olympia was full of men like these. Apart from the traders, who stood to make a lot of money during the journey to and from the Games and during the week they were there, the only people who could afford to come were the rich. They came to watch, to run their horses and chariots or to make alliances between neighbours and even old enemies. Some were there to find suitable husbands for their eligible daughters. It was a serious business—the Games were much more than just a sporting event.

Nic's stomach was rumbling but there were so many booths with such a variety of different foods he had difficulty picking out what he wanted. The crowd pulsed around him as Nic waited his turn patiently. He bought some bread and spicy meat and took a huge bite, swallowing greedily. The entire meal was gone in a moment, and still hunger gnawed away at the boy's stomach. A quick trip back to the booths again and he'd bought himself a honey cake as a special treat. They'd been Nic's favourite when Artemis was at home. She made them herself and teased him with them.

'No cake for you, Nic,' she'd say. 'Not until you fetch some fresh grapes for me.' He'd have run a hundred *stade* for one of Artemis's honey cakes. The sweet taste reminded Nicasylus of home so forcibly that hot tears stung suddenly, and he had to squeeze his eyes tightly to stop them from spilling; but nothing could prevent the sudden terrible rush of homesickness that washed over him in a tidal wave of grief and loss. Feelings that had been buried for ages bubbled to the surface of his mind and he couldn't keep them down any more. Nic found a space by the southern perimeter of the Altis and sat down, as he let everything rush uncontrollably through his mind and body. He wanted more than anything to be at home again. Nic buried his head in his arms and let the tears fall.

'What's up, lad?' The man he had met on the road stood above him. Nic wiped his face, hastily. He could feel the grime in streaks across his cheeks and his nose was running.

'Nothing.' He stared at the ground and willed the man to go away. The last thing he needed now was a thief to take an interest in him.

'You got a bit of food, I see. Can't be that you're hungry, then.' The man looked puzzled, as though he were really trying to understand. 'Are you sick?'

The truth was, he did feel sick. His stomach ached and he felt hot. Maybe he *was* sick.

'Yes.' Nic wiped his nose with the back of his hand.

'Well, have you got a spot picked out yet? Somewhere to lay your head tonight? Something to lay it on?' Nic shook his head. He had nothing. The thought of yet another night under the stars on a hard piece of ground made him feel desperate.

'Follow me, then. I'll share mine with you. You'll feel better tomorrow, no doubt.'

Reluctantly Nic followed. He had no better choice.

The man introduced himself as they walked. 'Amasis, from Stratus. I've come a long way to join in the festivities. So far, it's been a very profitable few days' work.' He winked at Nic like a fellow conspirator. 'You've done all right, have you? Apart from getting sick, that is.'

It was now or never. Nic took a deep breath.

'I'm not a thief. I'm Nicasylus of the house of Gorgias, goldsmith of Athens.'

Amasis laughed. 'Right. And my father was a general in Pericles' army. Oh, and I grow leeks for a living.'

'No. I really am. My stepfather sent me out of Athens when the plague started. The boat I was on was attacked by pirates and I was sold as a slave. I'm looking for a friend who's meant to be here, but I'm not sure if he's alive even.' Nic knew his explanation was practically incoherent. Amasis would never believe him.

Amasis was looking at Nic very thoughtfully. 'If you're not a thief, then how did you get that food in your hand?'

Nic stared down guiltily at the cake in his hand.

'I was given a purse by the captain of the boat that brought me to Patras.' Nic pulled it out and showed Amasis. The coins glinted in the strong sunlight and Amasis stared at them in absolute amazement.

'Look, it's true.' Nic flushed a deep red, right up his throat and across his whole face. He hated the idea that Amasis would think he had stolen this purse. 'He'd bought jewellery from my stepfather. The money was a gift from one Athenian to another.'

Amasis said nothing for a moment. He stared hard at Nic.

'I don't come from Athens. I can't be expected to know about your customs.' He frowned. 'So you're not a thief?'

'No, I'm not. I'm just trying to get home again.' A sudden, unexpected wave of nausea made Nic feel quite faint. There were terrible cramps in his stomach and he felt if he didn't sit down soon, there was a good chance he would fall down.

'I feel terrible,' he groaned. 'It must have been the meat I ate. I have to lie down soon.'

Amasis looked about him. He seemed to be searching for a good spot to stop. 'All right, Nicasylus of the house of Gorgias. I'll believe your story, though thousands wouldn't. You can rest here if you like.' They had reached the edge of the river, and even there was packed. Amasis gestured to a small tent. 'This is mine,' he said. 'There are a couple of skins in there. They'll hold you off the hard ground. Lie down and sleep. I'll wait outside.' With enormous gratitude, Nic pushed past and lay himself down on the skins. Relief at being prone again and a sense of absolute exhaustion combined. He shut his eyes and slept.

It was late in the evening when he was shaken awake roughly by a hand gripping his shoulder and a voice shouting in his ear.

'Hey! You! What do you think you're doing?'

Nic tried to focus his eyes. He could make out a face that wasn't Amasis's, and it looked angry.

'Amasis said this was his tent. He said to lie down.' It sounded stupid, even to Nic.

'You expect me to believe that? Get out, you little thief! Whoever Amasis is, this isn't his tent.' Nic was shoved through the door without ceremony.

'Wait!' Nic called. 'My purse is in there.'

'There's no purse in here except mine, so be on your way before I decide I was too easy on you.'

Nic couldn't believe what was happening. His head was spinning, his bowels felt as if they were going to erupt suddenly, his stomach was in spasm—and his purse was gone.

'Amasis,' he thought to himself. 'It must have been him. He put me here to steal my money.' But there was no way of finding the thief again in this crowd. At least, not tonight.

Nic found the communal pit. Afterwards he picked his way between bodies and tents to a small empty space on the rise that led away from the river, and settled himself on the ground. He stared at the night sky, rubbing his sore stomach gently as he lay. In a day it would be the full moon. The Games would begin with the triumphant procession of athletes from nearby Elis, where they had spent the last month in training, into the Altis. And Gellius would be among the athletes, Nic felt as certain of that as if he had already seen it. Amasis could keep the few coins he had stolen, and good luck to him.

The solemn sound of trumpeters woke him in the morning. The festival had already begun! Nic ran. In the Altis, he couldn't see a thing through the thicket of elbows and shoulders except the great altar to Zeus, where the sacred fire of white poplar wood had been burning for some time. Sweet smoke hung limply in the still, hot, olive grove. Over the low hum of the crowd came the sound of flautists, trumpets, voices chanting, the loud rumble of chariots, horses whinnying and snorting. The procession had already passed the innumerable altars that dotted the Altis, and it was almost at the altar of Zeus, where the Olympic judges, the Hellanodikai, would begin to sacrifice the hundreds of animals brought to honour the gods.

Nic wished he could see. In front of the chariots would be the competitors, and among them, perhaps, Gellius. Since he couldn't possibly get high enough to see over the shoulders of those around him, Nic went in the other direction. He tunnelled through the forest of legs, ignoring the howls of outrage or laughter from above. Eventually there was a space ahead of him big enough to stand up in.

He was directly in front of the altar and the Hellanodikai were mounting the steps, ready to sacrifice the first animal. They wore purple robes, a slice of the rainbow against the sea of white chitons that surrounded them. Nic tried to wriggle closer, but the crowd pushed back. A terrible sense of claustrophobia gripped him and he began to panic. He could hear the first sacrifice; the sudden squeal from the animal, and then the sigh that went up. The crowd seemed to expand with the energy of the kill. The legs of the steer, the most perfect part of the animal, would burn away to ash on the sacred fire to please Zeus. At tonight's feast, they could all enjoy a meal from the rest of the beast. A pungent, sweet odour of fresh blood and urine mingled with the smell of smoke.

Anxiety began to choke him; music merged with the sound of screaming animals and the drone of the priests and all he could think of was escape. He managed to move a short distance, up against the trunk of an ancient olive tree, where there was a tiny pocket of air and space. Nic looked up into the branches; easy to climb, and strong. He swung upwards and sat among the leafy canopy. Peering through the leaves was difficult, but he was above the crowd, he had air again.

A sight he could never have imagined, Olympia, home of the greatest games of all, was laid out in front of him. His father had been here once, stood out there and watched those sacrifices; he was following in his father's steps.

The crowd began to surge suddenly and he felt the tree sway with the movement. A flash of purple and the sound of trumpets signalled the procession moving off.

'Where are they all going?' he shouted down at a man who was struggling to get around the tree.

'The second half is about to begin in the Bouleu-terium. The swearing-in ceremony.' He looked surprised to find someone in the foliage above him. 'You're expected to be pure before you take part in the Games.' The man gestured towards the colourful building ahead of them, glittering in the early-morning sun. 'The athletes are about to be named in there.'

Nic shinned down the trunk. He really wanted to see this. Fear forgotten, he elbowed his way through the crush, which parted like water and let him through with no impediment. Nic could feel his muscles working as he pushed the crowd aside, his whole body felt alive. It made him want to shout with happiness. His clothes might be rags, and his money gone, but he was alive, and in Olympia! If only Tiso could have seen this.

The Bouleuterium was packed. It was a wonder anyone could see at all. All the athletes stood together as a boar was sacrificed. Together all the competitors swore on the entrails of the sacrificial animal that they had all undergone the compulsory nine months training for the Games, that they were indeed who they claimed to be, that they had committed no act of violence and that they would uphold all the rules of the Games. Then the Hellanodikai took their oaths, swearing to be impartial, to punish any competitor who failed to comply with the rules or broke his sacred oath, and to take no bribes.

'What would happen to anyone who tried to bribe the Hellanodikai?' Nic asked the man alongside him.

'Didn't you notice? The road here is lined with bronze statues of the gods. Paid for with fines for just that offence. And if a competitor lies about his worthiness, or when he takes the oath, he can be whipped. In front of everyone!'

'Oh.' Nic shuddered at the thought of being whipped in front of thousands of men. 'How could anyone survive humiliation like that?' Free men were never flogged. Only slaves were ever at the other end of the whip.

'Some men don't—the shame dogs them for the rest of their life. But if a man comes here and isn't pure of heart and mind and body, he isn't fit to compete. Simple as that. If he still enters the Games, he deserves whatever he gets.' The man paused. 'These games are not for men, but for the gods. They are our gift to them, and a gift given with deceit is unworthy of being given.'

Nic fell silent. From his hard-won position towards the front of the crowd, he waited impatiently. There were so many men to take the oath—was Gellius somewhere among them?

After the swearing-in came the drawing of lots to see who each athlete would compete against. A silver pot held tiny counters, and on each of these was a letter of the alphabet. For each event, athletes filed past and reached a hand into the pot. Their opponent was whoever drew the same letter. An endless stream of well-built, brown bodies streamed past the pot, groaning at their luck, or cheering aloud.

It was a long time before the Pankratiasts were called. Nic's head shot up. This was it. If Gellius didn't step forward to collect a marker, then he wasn't here.

CHAPTER

15

As Nic stuck his head up, he saw the back of the last contestant walking away with his marker. Something about the way the man moved was awfully familiar. He racked his brain for more information. Why did he feel he knew this man? Why did he feel suddenly afraid? He didn't know anybody who would be likely to compete in the Pankration, except Gellius. Nic dismissed the feeling, and turned to see Gellius himself step forward to collect his token.

Nic felt like weeping with happiness as he watched Gellius reach one huge hand into the silver pot and withdraw his marker, then step back and vanish among the group of athletes. The certainty that Gellius was safe filled Nic with a relief that was so extraordinary, it made him light-headed.

'He's one to watch for.' The man alongside was

almost talking to himself. 'Looks like a winner to me.'

'You can bet on it,' said Nic proudly. 'I know him. He's going to win, I'm sure of it.'

The other man smiled. It must have seemed ridiculous, Nic realised, that someone as filthy and ragged as himself would claim friendship with an Olympic competitor, but it was true. It was true, and no one could take that away.

The trumpeters' contest came next. A large number of heralds lined up hoping to out-do each other with fancy trills and long, quavering notes. Nic closed his eyes and listened. He felt more relaxed than he had since before he left Athens. There were five glorious summer days ahead of him, filled with the best in sport that the entire Greek world had to offer; his friend Gellius was here, and best of all he'd be going home soon.

When the ceremonies were finally over, Nic moved off with the rest of the crowd. He was determined to find Gellius and let him know he was there.

The athletes were all housed in their national groups on the northern side of the Altis at the foot of the hill of Cronos. Passing the food sellers again, Nic salivated at the smells that wafted across the space towards him. He kept walking; there was little danger of food poisoning without the money to buy the food! Anyway, Gellius would give him something to eat.

It wasn't possible to move through the crowd with

any speed so Nic gave up trying and slowed to the pace of those around him. Everywhere men were engaged in earnest conversations. He caught snippets in his own dialect as he walked along. The talk about Athens was still the plague, how devastating it had been, how many businesses had been ruined, how many good men had died. Nic found himself wondering whether it was possible that Mother and Gorgias and Artemis died too. It was a thought he didn't want to have, and it was followed by another. What if Gellius were embarrassed to have him turn up unannounced like this—filthy and hungry and needing money and a place to sleep? After all, they'd only known each other one single night. For the first time since he'd set out, Nic was really, truly afraid. If Gellius abandoned him, then he was lost.

At the athletes' compound, he hesitated.

'What are you after?' a voice boomed, so loudly Nic almost choked.

'I'm looking for Gellius, of Athens. Competitor in the Pankration.' Nic tried to muster all the authority he could find, but his voice still wavered.

'And what does someone like you want with an Olympic competitor?' There was no mistaking the disgust in the man's voice.

'I'm a friend of his,' Nic began. 'He'll want to see me. I think.'

'You think! Well, *I* don't. And *I* say you high-tail

it out of here, my lad, before I call someone to throw you out. The athletes mustn't be disturbed. Get off! Back wherever you came from.'

'But I have to see him.' Nic was begging, and ashamed of it. 'I've got no money and he'll look after me until we get back to Athens. I know he will.'

A look of annoyance flitted across the man's face. 'Here, catch.' He tossed a small coin at Nic. 'Take it and buy yourself some food. And stay away from this area if you know what's good for you. Gellius won't want to be seeing the likes of you, and nor do I.'

Reluctantly, Nic caught the coin and turned away. He wished he could throw it back again, but the truth was that if he couldn't get in to see Gellius, he needed every scrap he could come by.

'Thanks,' he muttered under his breath, 'For nothing.'

The man had heard him. 'Ungrateful wretch!' he shouted behind Nic.

But Nic didn't care. He felt as if he were back where he'd started from; alone, friendless and without any money. And all because some busybody thought he wasn't fit to see Gellius.

He'd get as clean as he could and try again. It was just a matter of coming back more presentable, at another time, when that man wasn't there. The place wasn't guarded, it couldn't be too hard. Nic wandered back through the crowd again, looking for Amasis.

The robbery still rankled. If he managed to find Amasis, Nic decided, he'd have no hesitation in stealing back his money.

From the Stadium came the sounds of the crowd, cheering on contestants in the boys' races, but Nic didn't bother to look. All he cared about right now was finding somewhere to wash and then getting some food into his belly. He headed back towards the River Alpheus, found a relatively quiet spot and stripped off his filthy chiton. Nobody paid any attention to him at all. Waist-deep in the slow-moving water, he scrubbed and scraped with angry vigour to get rid of the grime that had stained his skin brown for weeks. Nic thumped the wet chiton up and down on the rocks, until it began to look as if it might fall apart. Washing wasn't something he'd ever been taught to do. He wished he'd watched the slaves back home in Athens to see how they kept his clothes clean. What he ended up with was a garment that looked as if it had survived a muddy avalanche and been shredded by sharp stones on the way. He laid it across the lower branches of a tree on the river bank, then sat huddled alongside, naked. It was so hot that his body dried off in a few minutes. The chiton took longer, and in the end he put it on damp. Dressed again, Nic wandered slowly back across the field towards the food sellers. This time he would be a lot more careful about what he ate.

The first day passed into evening. Fires were

126

burning on sacrificial altars in the Altis and the olive trees threw fantastic shadows against the walls of the Temple of Zeus. There was no point in trying to find Gellius tonight, Nic decided; best to wait for morning. With any luck, he might catch him on his way to the Great Gymnasium for training sessions.

In the east the moon was rising. It slowly filled the sky, obliterating the first faint stars and tinging every tiny detail of Olympia with a golden light. He remembered watching a moon just like this, with Gellius, on the deck of the boat.

'See that?' Gellius had said. 'That's an Olympic moon. Next year, as that moon rises over the horizon, I'll be in the Altis at Olympia.'

It felt like a lifetime ago. Nic settled himself on the grass and looked around him.

Olympia was a small enough place, but it had a special charm that was rare in Greece. Instead of harsh, stony mountains, the site was edged by water; the River Alpheus, which threaded its way through rich flood plains, and its northern tributary, the River Cladeus. Olympia was nestled in the narrow angle between these shallow waterways with some low, broken hills behind. Nic was on the tranquil lower slope of the hill of Cronos looking down towards the flat ground of the Altis. A forest of altars and statues and graceful white buildings—all honey-coloured now in the moonlight—were dotted across the landscape.

Around him, and throughout the field, were huge old olive trees, the white underbelly of their dull green leaves shivering golden as a light wind raked through them. A spiderweb of bright shadows flickered and trembled against everything. What ground was left uncovered by tents or men or market booths was awash with tiny white chamomile flowers, already beginning to be trampled down by the unremitting stamp of so many feet. The flowers perfumed the night air with a fragrance so subtle it was easily drowned out by the sharper notes of the wood fires and the smell of too many people.

Nic took a deep breath and tried to take it all in at once. Olympia was a place the gods would love. He understood why the ancients had chosen this heavenly site.

The sounds of feasting and laughter and movement began to die down as everyone turned in for the night. At the crack of dawn tomorrow, the whole place would shake itself awake; each man trying to get down to the Hippodrome as quickly as possible, before all the best vantage points were taken. By sunrise one of the most popular events of the week, chariot racing, would have begun.

'Maybe I'll just have a quick peek at the first heat,' Nic thought sleepily. 'It'd be a shame to come this far and not see a chariot race.' He nodded his head as if agreeing with himself, and closed his eyes.

128

this point that the riders would find the rising sun in their eyes, with time for only a few more turns of the wheel before they had to brace themselves for the dangerous bend at the end of the Hippodrome. Only the best drivers managed to get round without crashing here, by urging on their outside horse and at the same time reining in the horse closest to the inside. The less able drivers would fail, spinning out on the turn, reducing the chariots to a more manageable number.

He missed the start because his attention was diverted for a moment by the unexpected sight of Amasis, no more than a few paces away. He was clearly working the spectators, thieving whatever he could in the jostling and shoving. Nic slipped into the crowd behind him. Amasis was making his way up the embankment, through the thickest part of the throng and down the other side leading away from the Hippodrome. Surely he hadn't run out of people to rob? Puzzled, Nic followed at a short distance, careful not to let the thief out of his sight. Below the Hippodrome the land ran gently down towards the river. Amasis, a bundle in his hand that looked like a large purse, headed directly for the road that ran beside it. Nic hesitated: should he keep following, and see if he could possibly get his money back somehow, at the risk of missing the chariot race, the most exciting event of all? But there should be time for both; there were still more heats before the real chariot racing started. He decided to follow Amasis. He wanted the satisfaction of stealing back what had belonged to him in the first place.

The sun was well and truly up over the horizon before Amasis paused. Already it was a hot day, Nic wished he had water with him. Ahead, the thief drank greedily from a skin, letting the water run down his chin and over his bare neck. It was all Nic could do not to leap out then and there, snatch the water and the purse and run back. But he didn't. Chances were Amasis would catch him before he got halfway. There were really only two choices—be straightforward and ask for his money, or be dishonest and steal it at the first opportunity, then run as if all the gods were on his tail.

His opportunity came sooner than he expected. As the River Cladeus dropped away from the plain, it cut steep gorges. Amasis left the track and made his way towards these cliffs. Nic slipped from tree to tree as he shadowed the thief. Close to the river, Amasis vanished. One moment he was there, the next he was gone. Nic hesitated. To leave the security of the trees might mean being caught and having to explain exactly what he was doing out here, right behind Amasis. He decided to wait and hide. Less than five minutes later, Amasis reappeared and this time headed back towards Olympia, without the purse in his hands.

Nic couldn't believe his luck. It made such perfect

sense he was surprised he hadn't thought of it earlier. Amasis couldn't afford to keep his dishonest earnings anywhere in Olympia where they might be found. It would be death for him. There must be a cave somewhere in the trees ahead, deep enough and reasonably well hidden, so that Amasis could use it as his safe spot.

As Amasis passed, he came so close Nic could smell him; rank and sour like the wolf all those weeks ago. Nic waited until the thief had vanished around a bend in the road, then darted forward. The opening was a few paces in front of him, well hidden by boulders and debris from fir and olive trees piled up against it as if a storm had blown everything there. No one who wasn't looking for it would ever have found it easily. Nervously Nic stepped inside. It was much darker than he expected. He had to feel his way along with his fingers, sliding them over the rough, damp walls and probing with his outstretched feet to make sure he didn't trip. Somewhere in here Amasis had hidden his stolen money, and that meant Nic's purse was here as well. He was going to find it, no matter what. About thirty paces in, his foot stubbed against something hard on the sandy floor of the cave. In the murky shadow, he reached down and felt around. Immediately his fingertips touched a large heavy, leather pouch. Nic laughed, and straightened up, the purse in his hand.

'I've got you now, Amasis!'

An arm locked suddenly around Nic's chest, and a rough hand pressed a blade against his throat.

'So sorry. Actually, it's the other way around. *I've got you.*'

Nic's body froze.

'There's something very comforting about the way boys behave. So predictable. You were almost too easy to catch, a willing fly drawn by the promise of a little honey.' The steel of the knife smelt like vinegar under his nose. It twitched against Nic's skin as if it had a life of its own. 'Now you just stay quiet, my lad, and nothing bad will happen. I've got to keep you here for a few days. It's a bit dark, and at night the mosquitoes try to carry you away, but at least this way you stay alive.'

'Why are you doing this to me?' Nic gasped. He could hardly breathe, 'I'm no threat to you. And anyway, you can find another hiding place. I won't tell!'

'You misunderstand, lad. It would be very dangerous indeed for you to show your face at all. You've got important enemies in Olympia and they don't want to see you there any more. I've been paid to dispose of you.'

Nic had no idea what he was talking about.

'I don't know anyone at Olympia except Gellius. You're making a mistake, you've got the wrong person, Amasis.'

'Now that's where *you're* wrong.' Amasis pushed

Nic to the ground onto his stomach, and began looping a rope around the boy's wrists and ankles, trussing him like a bird. He pulled tight, so Nic's head snapped back towards his feet. 'It's a good thing I've got a heart of gold. I'm not going to kill you.' The rope looped around his waist and tied at the back. 'I'll let you go as soon as the Games are over and the crowd's left.'

'You're wrong. It's not me you want. Please!'

'You'll be all right here. I'll leave you water, and if you're good, I'll come back tonight with food. But when I let you go, you'd better keep your mouth shut about all this, if you want to stay breathing.'

'This is crazy! You have to let me go. I need to find Gellius and get back to Athens with him. I don't have any enemies. And I don't know anyone else at the Games. Nobody!' Nic was shouting. His voice bounced around the walls of the cave.

'I wouldn't bellow too loudly if I were you,' cautioned Amasis. 'These old caves are prone to collapse if there's a loud enough noise.' He tipped Nic over so that he lay on his side, within reach of the water skin. 'You won't starve till I get here tonight. Have a good day.'

His footsteps disappeared as absolutely as a stone disappears into water. Gone. And Nic was alone, in a dark hole, again.

CHAPTER

17

It was worse than anything that had happened to him since he left Athens. Tears threatened to spill down his cheeks but this time Nic wouldn't let them. For a while, he lay in that uncomfortable position without moving. Whatever strength and common sense he possessed would be needed now. This was not a time for futile struggling, this was a time for intelligence and courage.

'Think like an athlete,' Nic told himself. 'You'll win this bout, it's just a matter of how. There *is* a way out of this hole. Concentrate.'

He felt the strength of the bonds around his wrists and feet. The rope was thin, but strong, and he couldn't feel any rough or jagged rock behind him that he could use as a saw. There was no slackness at all, so it was impossible to loosen the rope either—Amasis had

done a good job of tying him up. Nic tried to relax.
The darkness of the cave had become less solid; he
could faintly make out the walls and the sandy floor.
He was able to wriggle enough to form a gentle
depression in the sand for his body, and that gave
him some comfort. The sand was clean and cool and
soft—he could be thankful for that much. It was better
than the stinking hold of the pirate ship.

Thirst returned very quickly. Nic managed to drink
some of the precious water, by pressing his face against
the sand and grasping the spout on the skin with his
teeth. With each mouthful he swallowed sand, but that
was a small price to pay. It quenched his thirst and
made him feel much calmer. Nic wished Amasis had
at least left him upright. On his side he felt completely
helpless.

'Who wants me gone?' He spoke out loud, just for
the company of his own voice. There was no answer,
of course. He had no idea who could possibly have
paid Amasis to kill him. Nic shuddered. It was too
much to think about. What if they'd chosen someone
else? Perhaps a thief who had no compunction about
murdering anybody? Amasis was many things, but
apparently not a killer. There was not a single reason
that Nic could think of that would make anyone want
to keep him from the Games. Surely he was no more
important than any other spectator at the events? More
questions than answers chased each other round in his

136

head until he felt like his brain was scrambled. From the time he'd left Athens his life had been so extraordinary, nothing was inconceivable any more.

Nic lost any sense of time. He slept in fits and starts, ignoring his hunger and drinking from the skin repeatedly. His arms and legs were so stiff from the unnatural position he was in that they had lost all sensation. He tried rolling from side to side to get his circulation going, but it made little difference. One side of his body was a dead weight; he couldn't even feel his fingers or toes any more. He tried to keep his spirits up by reciting poetry he'd learnt at school in Athens, along with snatches of old songs that Artemis had taught him.

Once he imagined he heard a flute and the faint resonant melody soothed him so much he actually forgot where he was and drifted in a gentle sea of memories. All the time he had been gone from Athens he had been so preoccupied with surviving that there had been precious little time for thoughts of home, and besides, thoughts like these had always made things worse for him. Now he let his mind meander through those images of his mother and Gorgias and Artemis; all so real it almost felt as if he were there with them still.

It could have been days or hours, there was no way of telling which, when Amasis reappeared suddenly, a burning torch in his hand.

'Here you go. Some food for you.'

He shoved the torch into the sand and squatted down. 'I'm afraid it's not hot any more. There were such rich pickings in the crowd on the way out, I couldn't help myself. It delayed me and your dinner got cold.' He chuckled. 'I don't suppose you care either way, do you? You're probably pretty hungry by now.' He began to break off lumps of the meat in his hands and shovel them into Nic's mouth.

The boy's hunger was so overwhelming that he almost choked on the first mouthful. It was too difficult to sit up, so he had to make do with eating the food on his side, fed from the thief's dirty fingers.

'How long have I been here?' Nic asked through a mouthful of beans and corn.

Amasis coughed. 'Details, mere details. Still, I don't suppose there's much to do in the dark, is there? Except watch the hours go by. Eat up, I haven't got all day. There's work to do.' He pushed the last morsel into Nic's mouth and stood up. 'I'll be off now. I don't want to give the mosquitoes a meal too, they can have a feed off you instead.'

'Amasis!' Nic's bladder was bursting. 'You have to untie me, I need to piss.'

'The sand will soak it up. I don't have time right now. I'm missing the feast. I'll be back later tonight, I'll have a bit of stuff to stash by then.' Amasis and his light vanished.

A terrible wail reverberated round the walls of the cave. 'Come back! Come back!' Nic screamed, but there was no answer. He peed right where he lay. The relief was enormous, and he wondered why he'd waited so long to do it. He struggled to make his mind work properly. Amasis had said he'd be late for the feast. There was a ritual banquet in the evening of the third day. Had Nic been in here for a day and a half? Was that possible? If he had, then tomorrow was the Pankration.

Nic struggled frantically, trying to loosen the ropes around his feet and hands. The ropes slid slightly but no matter what he did, the bonds were not even a fraction looser. Huddled and beaten, he slumped on the floor of the cave. Nothing he had encountered so far had been as bad as this. Imprisonment, being tied up like an animal and left alone in the dark for days on end—it was unbearable.

He made an enormous effort to marshal his thoughts, but his mind refused to co-operate. Nic began to say aloud the last lesson he could remember. The class had been learning a poem by Pindar, from his Olympian Odes. He struggled for the words.

gold shines
like a burning fire in the night above all proud wealth.

The dream he'd had on the boat to Patras came

139

back to him. He'd dreamt of a beautiful olive grove, full of temples and statues, where he must step forward and tell the truth, even though it put his life in danger. He knew where the grove was now. It was the Altis in Olympia. Something was going to happen at the Altis in Olympia. Nic had no idea what it was, but he knew he had to be there when it happened.

Calm, like the eye of a hurricane, settled upon him. A sense of purpose and courage returned as Nic lay trussed like a chicken in the dark. A wonderful plan had sprung fully formed into his mind. It depended on Amasis behaving predictably, but then, Nic decided, there was no reason to expect he wouldn't.

The drone of the mosquitoes was almost friendly; he let them feed off his blood. There was nothing he could do to stop them. Not yet.

CHAPTER

18

A few hours later, the merry jingling of gold and silver and a loud, drunken song reverberated through the cave. Amasis had returned, and clearly it had been a profitable night.

'This izzn a social visit, m'boy.' Amasis giggled like a child. He stuck the torch deep into the sand, filling the chamber with a sudden dancing light that blinded Nic for a few moments.

'S'bit bright for you, m'fren?' the thief chortled. His voice was thick and faintly slurred, he was having difficulty focussing on his young prisoner's face. 'Juzz dropping off some goods, for *safe* keeping with *you.*' He laughed and sat down with a thump. 'Missed a great banquet, you did.' He started to sing loudly and tunelessly but with a great deal of vigour, slapping his hand against his thigh to keep the beat.

141

'I really need you to untie me, Amasis. I'm so cramped I can't feel my legs. Please.'

'Noway.' Amasis shook his head vehemently. 'Noway. Can't do that. Noway.' He settled himself alongside Nic, and nudged him in the ribs. 'Your fren looks good in training sessions. Won't win, though.'

'Gellius? What do you mean? Why won't he win?'

Amasis leaned forward towards Nic and whispered. 'S'others who want to win. Badly. Your fren's too soft. Izzn mean enough.'

'Why not? Who's he fighting?'

'Noway. Won't say. Not sure, anyway.' Amasis was sounding more slurred. 'Tired. Need a sleep.' With a soft snoring sound, as if a blanket had smothered him, Amasis stretched out on the floor and closed his eyes. In a moment, his breathing was deep, slow and steady. Nic watched the man carefully, it wouldn't do for him to wake up suddenly now. He wanted to be absolutely certain that Amasis was quite unconscious. His plan depended on it.

'There's something so predictable about a drunk.' Nic laughed. 'You really should have stayed sober, my friend.' With great difficulty he manoeuvred his body towards the torch and let it lick at the ropes around his wrists, burning his flesh as well. Nic put up with the pain for as long as he could by thinking of the Pankration. Gellius could withstand much worse than this, he reminded himself. When it became too much,

142

he rolled over and quenched his blistered wrists in the cool sand, rolling them over each other, rubbing away raw skin and hurting more than Nic had imagined was possible, but weakening the charred ropes to thin, frayed strands. Nic strained against his bonds and felt them snap, with a discharge of energy that shot though his body as if he were a bow releasing its arrow. The relief was enormous; he lifted his head and stretched his neck and shoulders forward. He needed to turn his entire body in the opposite direction to the one it had endured for so long.

It took quite a few minutes for him to get the burnt ropes off his wrists and then untie his ankles. There was no strength in his fingers. He had to stretch and flex and bend and walk around on his hands and knees for a while before he started to feel normal again. Sensation returned to his fingertips first; he could feel the blood flooding back through his body.

It should have been a simple matter to tie the thief up, except Nic's fingers were so stiff he could barely hold the pieces of rope. Amasis didn't stir once while he was being trussed, just snored and sighed a little. When Nic had finished, he walked shakily towards the entrance of the cave. It took a while; the path was winding and narrow, he was unsteady on his feet, and water had more shape than his muscles did just then. The night sky, when he finally reached the opening, was so bright it was like walking out into daylight.

The moon was an enormous orb illuminating the entire landscape. An Olympic moon. Exactly what he needed.

It was a long walk back to the Games. By the time he reached Olympia, the place was utterly still. A few sacrificial fires still smouldered, but nothing moved. Nic made his way silently among the tents, and positioned himself in front of the Gymnasium. He would sleep there for what remained of the night, and in the morning he would find Gellius.

The newly risen sun streaming through the grove woke Nic. Athletes, all giant men, either Pankratiasts or Pentathletes, were going past without so much as a sideways glance. Nic got to his feet and hid himself behind an olive tree. Maybe he would recognise whoever it was who wanted him dead, or even better, find Gellius. Not a single familiar face passed by. In the arena the first heats in Wrestling had already begun, cheered on by a mighty crowd of enthusiastic onlookers. It took quite a while to get there and the whole way Nic dodged and weaved among the men and the trees, trying to keep a low profile and at the same time search the crowd. It was no good. Gellius was not among them. The last place to look was the training area. It was on the other side of the Altis and there were fewer people there; Nic managed to slip inside without anyone noticing him. The very first person he saw was Gellius.

'Gellius!' Relief and happiness flooded through Nic. The captain stood right in front of him, staring.

'Nicasylus? Is that you?'

'It's me, Gellius.'

There was an extraordinary moment when they stood without speaking, staring and staring, then at the same moment they grabbed each other and hugged and danced around the floor.

'I don't believe it!' Gellius was trying to take in how big Nic was, and how his face had changed. He held Nic at arms length. 'You're hardly a boy any more. How did you get here? What happened to you?'

The two sat down on a bench in the Gymnasium and began to share their histories since that last dreadful night on the boat. It was a haphazard retelling of events. First Gellius would break in, then Nic. They exclaimed over each other's stories, and laughed and cried together. Nic was about to tell the captain about Amasis and his capture, when Gellius suddenly blurted out, 'I found your sister when I got back to Athens, Nic.'

'Artemis! She's well?'

'She survived the plague, her husband didn't. Your stepfather and your mother died. I'm so sorry.'

It took a few moments for the information to sink in. Nic's eyes grew bright with tears.

'Artemis is longing to see you. She's miserable in her father-in-law's house. It's draining the life out of her while she waits there for an offer of marriage.' Gellius looked flushed. 'Your sister's very beautiful. She should have no difficulty finding a husband.' He looked at the ground.

Nic looked sideways at his friend. Gellius was brick-red.

'And who is this?' Porinus stood in front of them, smiling. 'Don't tell me, let me guess. This is your little lost friend, Nicasylus.'

'Not so little any more, and no longer lost!' Gellius stood up. 'Nic, this is my oldest friend, and my trainer, Porinus.'

The two shook hands solemnly.

'What a pleasure to find you alive, young man. With *one* less thing on his mind, Gellius will have a much greater chance of winning,' said Porinus, dryly.

Nic looked quizzically at Gellius, who threw his head back and roared with laughter.

'He's trying to say that I've had my mind on other things. Maybe I have. But it's wonderful to find you again. Look, I have to train. My event is this afternoon. You'll be there?'

'There's nowhere else I'd want to be!' Nic stood and Gellius hugged him.

'Not too big for a hug yet. That's good to see. You'll have to look after yourself, I'm afraid. Porinus will have to stay with me for the rest of the time until the match. You'll be all right?' Nic nodded. 'Don't vanish again, will you!' With a smile and a clap of one huge hand across Nic's back, the captain strode out into the arena towards the punching bag.

Porinus motioned Nicasylus towards the bench again.

'Wait here and watch, if you like, Nic. I'll be over there helping Gellius.' Porinus stepped away, a look of concern creasing his forehead. 'Keep your shoulder down when you do that, Gellius. Remember?' He was already walking across the floor.

Nic stood up. He hadn't had a chance to tell either of them about the last few days. A shudder ran down his spine and for a second he felt immensely vulnerable. Any one of the men milling around right now in the Gymnasium could be the man who wanted him dead. He still didn't understand why—it just didn't make sense for anyone to think that a boy like him was a threat. Still, just to be on the safe side, it might be best to keep a low profile.

Despite wanting to watch Gellius train, for the rest of the morning Nic hid. He could hear great shouts coming from the direction of the Wrestling competition, but resisted the temptation to go and watch. Nic even stayed away from the Pentathlon, an event he had always wanted to see. Instead he found himself a cubbyhole among the rubble left over from the building of the Temple of Zeus, and stayed there until the Pankration was called. Careful to keep his head down, he slipped among the crowd and wriggled to the front in order to get a better view. The oath-taking ceremony was about to begin. All the Pankratiasts were lined up, laughing and chatting easily with one another. Nic was just in time to hear the first name called loudly.

'Cadmus of Amantia, son of Phayllus,' the herald announced. 'Competitor in the Pankration.' A handsome, smiling man stepped forward with an easy swagger. He looked like anyone Nic might have met along his travels: like a rich man who wanted to win glory for his city.

The Pankratiast who called himself Cadmus stood facing the crowd, and Nic actually felt his heart skip a beat. He recognised the man immediately. Not his face, he'd never seen that. It was his feet that gave him away. Six toes.

In front of the statue of Zeus Horkias, the protector of oaths, stood a man who was not fit to compete in the greatest games of all. Nic half expected to see the thunderbolts in the statue's hands spring to life and sizzle across the short space that separated them, striking down the impostor. But nothing happened. No one stepped forward and denounced Cadmus, if that was really the pirate's name. More likely it was the name of one of his victims, who was by now a slave far away from here. Nic began to shiver, despite the oppressive heat. His skin felt clammy and his pulse raced. The pirate captain swore to all and sundry that he was without blemish, that he was entitled to compete, and not a single voice was raised against him. It was no wonder he'd wanted to get rid of Nic. He must have seen him and realised that Nic was the only person there who might be able to identify him for the murderer he was. He probably didn't realise that Nic had never actually seen his face at all.

'Liar!' Nic wanted to shout. 'This man is a liar! He sold me into slavery and killed the men who tried to stop him.' But nothing came out of his mouth. He couldn't challenge Cadmus. It was a crime to accuse an athlete without strong proof; the fact that someone had six toes on one foot wasn't proof of anything and he couldn't claim to recognise the man any other way.

When the herald finished, Cadmus smiled, and stepped aside, blending in again with all the other athletes. Nic's blood was boiling. He had never felt so powerless in his whole life. He let himself vanish back into the crowd a little, his enemy less than a few paces away.

The next competitor was called.

'Gellius of Athens, son of Hermes,' the herald's voice was loud and clear. 'Competitor in the Pankration!'

From behind the wall of onlookers, Nic cheered with all the others as Gellius stepped forward to take the oath. He could just see the captain, standing there steady as a rock; feet apart, head high; his big, powerful body and his honest face reflecting the true values of Olympia. No one there could possibly have doubted him. Gellius repeated the oath in a clear, strong voice. There were no challenges—he stepped back into the crowd and was lost from Nic's view. It was too late now to stop Cadmus, Nic knew. The moment to speak out had been lost. He had ignored the warning in his dream, his fear had sealed the captain's fate.

'Please,' Nic prayed, 'let Gellius win.' But there was no answer.

CHAPTER

19

In front of the altar of Zeus in the Altis, a large muddy circle had been prepared. It was bounded by a deep channel that at once kept the wet clay from oozing out and kept the spectators from encroaching on the fight space. An official stood to one side, holding a long thin rod with a forked end and carefully watching every movement. There were only two rules in this competition: no biting, or gouging eyes. The rod would fall hard on a competitor who broke the rules.

The two men were circling each other with all the angry energy of fighting bulls, sparring savagely in front of a crowd that was already wild with excitement. The Pankration was what most of the onlookers had come to Olympia to see; the strongest men in Greece fighting each other, bare-fisted and unarmed, until one or other of them surrendered or died. This was blood sport and definitely not for the faint-hearted.

A cheer went up: the first fall had taken place! Two huge men, already dripping with sweat, wrestled each other in the mud, pushing the limits of human endurance as they twisted each other's bodies and bent arms, legs and necks into unnatural and incredibly painful positions. The object of the Pankration was to inflict so much pain on your opponent that he would surrender. This first heat was one of four. The victor in each would go on to fight again, two elimination bouts before the match for the olive wreath. The last Pankratiast able to withstand his opponent's vicious blows would emerge the winner. Gellius was competing against a man called Morsimus from Crete in the fourth heat, Cadmus against someone else in the third heat.

Porinus was right at ringside, watching everything with an avid interest. Either of these men could ultimately be Gellius's opponent. He wanted to see how they fought and make note of any unusual techniques or holds, so that Gellius could be prepared.

'I can't watch!' Nic spoke aloud without thinking, covering his eyes as a scream of pain went up from one of the Pankratiasts whose left arm was locked high above his neck, while his opponent straddled his back and sank his free fist into the man's kidneys. Nic couldn't bear to think of Gellius in a fight like this. It

152

had seemed different when Gellius described it; more honourable somehow. Nic hadn't expected this knock-'em-down-and-drag-'em-out style of fight. He could never be a Pankratiast after watching this.

Already the two men in the mud-pit were bloody from open wounds to head and body. Their hair hung in saturated strings and their naked bodies were streaked with mud and bright red where a fist had connected forcefully. They looked more like animals than men.

Nic wriggled back out of the crowd. Too much of this and he'd be sick, it would be better to wait until Gellius was actually fighting. In his cubbyhole near the temple of Zeus, Nic curled up like a baby. Anger and fear tumbled over each other in a relentless cycle inside his head. Anger that the pirate was going to get away with his lies, and fear that because of it Gellius would lose. The memory of those feet flooded back, how they had looked somehow like lethal weapons, not just ordinary toes. This man was a killer, and he enjoyed his work. He'd have no hesitation fighting dirty, Nic was sure of that. Gellius, no matter how good a Pankratiast he was, would be no match for a man with a soul so black.

How Cadmus had come to be here, and why, were mysteries. Coming to Olympia seemed an enormous risk to take for a man who made his living from murdering, thieving and slave-trading. But then, every

153

Pankratiast risked his life to compete. The glory of winning was everything to men like these.

The roars of the crowd around the Pankration heats rose like flames leaping from a wildfire. Each time the throng shouted, it signalled a corresponding vicious blow that would have sent one of the contestants into a frenzy of pain. The tumult would act like a spur and drive the injured athlete to even greater feats of endurance, helping both men inflict even worse pain. Perhaps this was why Cadmus had come, to hear cheers of encouragement when he inflicted pain on another man. Maybe that was what he needed.

Hunger drove Nic out eventually. He made his way back to the food stalls and as brazenly as if he had been born to a life of thievery, stole bread and some meat threaded onto skewers. It was easy. He ate them slowly, savouring each mouthful and wiping his chin with his hand. The sun was high in the sky now, time to return to the Pankration—much as Nic wished he didn't have to watch.

It was a terrible shock to get to the front of the crowd and discover Gellius and Cadmus confronting each other; circling like wild beasts who knew that one false move could be their last.

'What happened?' he asked someone. 'What heat is this?'

'Two contestants won their match, but were badly injured. They couldn't fight each other.' The man shrugged. 'A pity, but it happens. These two were the only ones left. This bout is for the olive wreath.'

'What?' Nic could hardly believe it. It was his worst fear realised. Reluctantly he positioned himself near the edge of the pit, close to Porinus, who was urging Gellius on with shouts, his fists flying around in the air in front of him like loose arrows.

Gellius could feel the strength in his feet and hands and his entire body. He was as completely centred as it was possible to be. He filled his lungs in strong, slow, rhythmic breaths that made him calm and unafraid. Every muscle was alive and full of blood, ready to flex or relax at a moment's notice. His abdomen tensed and his fists balled.

On the other side of the pit, circling cautiously was his opponent. Of the two, Gellius was the lighter, but he had speed and agility on his side. He'd watched the earlier heat and noticed that Cadmus relied on his weight to force the man to the ground. Once his opponent was down, he had the advantage.

From the opposite side of the pit, Cadmus smiled; a sneer that transformed his face from handsome to hateful in a split second. Something about the man sent a chill through Gellius. Cadmus had beaten his challenger in the earlier heat, by crippling him. The crowd had booed, but the most elite of athletes had

had to be carried off with his leg dangling, useless and broken, and Cadmus had watched, looking very pleased. Here was a contestant who competed, not for the greatest glory of the gods and to honour his city of birth, but for his own sake. For his own ends. Gellius forced himself to focus.

With no warning, a six-toed foot, as hard as granite, appeared from nowhere. There was no time to swivel. Gellius took the blow direct to the chest and found himself thrust violently backwards, pain knifing through him. As he staggered, Cadmus struck. Gellius felt his right arm being pulled almost out of its socket as he was dragged towards Cadmus, and spun round like a top. He tried to stay upright as Cadmus's left arm snaked under his armpit and behind his neck, forcing his head down and arm back, maintaining a grip so excruciating that Gellius bellowed like a lion.

'Keep your feet!' Porinus was screaming from the sidelines. 'Don't let him get you on the ground!'

Gellius closed his eyes for a second and saw himself slipping free from the hold. Like a knot tied in butter he slid right through and pivoted somehow in the tiny space left to him. The release of pain and the sudden rush of blood back to his neck was a relief beyond words.

Nic was leaping about like a mad thing, cheering. It was like watching a dancer, not a Pankratiast. The crowd went wild, and so did Cadmus. He never hesitated, but rushed like a bull, head down, shoulders set like a battering ram, straight into Gellius's belly, knocking him backwards again with enormous force. The two men toppled over together, locked in that fierce squeeze. Somehow Gellius managed to maintain his balance and plant his feet, pushing forward at the same time as he landed a mighty punch to the upper body. The dull thud of fist and abdomen were like music to Nic's ears now.

'Kill him!' someone was screaming close by. 'Kill him!'

It wasn't clear who should be killed, and maybe it didn't matter. Cadmus roared; his eyes were wild. A barrage of bare-fisted blows rained down on Gellius, kidney punches, each of them like a rock slamming into him and sending pain ricocheting along every nerve in his lower body. He struggled to land a single blow on Cadmus, who seemed impervious to any kind of hit, taking each one as if he were made of sand and never faltering in his own vicious onslaught.

'Get away, Gellius, move back!' Porinus's shouts fell on deaf ears. As the two men struggled close, Cadmus scraped his fingers roughly against the soft tissue of his opponent's eyes. His body shielded the move from the umpire, who tried to get in close to see what was happening. Gellius screamed and swung his head away in a rapid movement that caused the pirate's fingernail to scrape right through the skin of his cheek, so that a river of blood poured down his face and into his open mouth. The excruciating pain sent Gellius into a momentary spin. He tried to shield his eyes from a further blow and Cadmus, sensing the advantage brought his whole forehead down like a stone in a violent head butt that sent the captain reeling in surprise and agony.

Cadmus went in for the kill, a backwards kick straight at his opponent's head that only managed to connect on the very tip of the chin. By some absolute miracle, Gellius had managed again to spin out of the way and at the same moment he grasped Cadmus's foot and threw him over onto the ground. A shout went up that exceeded anything Nic had ever heard—a giant voice, screaming for blood.

The men on the ground were oblivious now to the crowd, or the place, or why they were there. A fundamental instinct had taken over. They rolled around like a single spring. Grappling with each other until they were on their knees, heads and shoulders locked, pushing and shoving backwards and forwards with tremendous force. Cadmus slipped in the mud and Gellius knew instinctively that this was his best chance. If he were ever going to win, it had to be now. This was it. This was what all his years of training were for.

With a mighty roar, Gellius spun behind Cadmus

and drove his knee into the man's back, knocking him sprawling to the ground—was on top before Cadmus had a chance to do more than get to his knees. With his whole body he drove the pirate down towards the ground, and at the same time, clamped his thigh over Cadmus's leg in a vine lock. Two naked men in the absolute prime of their lives, one twined round the other like a strangler fig. A wonderful lightness of being, a sense of elation, filled Gellius. He could taste victory over this dirty fighter.

Cadmus was off balance, his right arm was being forced back up behind him so far it had to snap any second, and Gellius was a dead weight forcing his left shoulder to the floor. Any second Nic expected to hear the sound of bones snapping as Cadmus collapsed, but instead the pirate somehow folded like a pack of cards, and rolled out from underneath onto his back. Nic screamed and Gellius fell sideways. The roar of the crowd was like a whip. In seconds he had regained his feet. Gellius fell on the pirate again but Cadmus shot out his left leg and stopped the rush, his six toes spreadeagled rigidly across the captain's chest.

It was a brilliant manoeuvre. Gellius, momentarily checked, grabbed the leg with his left hand, and pushed down hard on Cadmus's neck with his right. He could hear the sound of the vertebrae in the pirate's upper spine cracking and yet Cadmus uttered not a single whimper. Instead he grabbed Gellius by the

159

ankle; clearly he hoped to rip the ankle from its socket, but he couldn't apply any pressure, his elbow was losing its grip on the ground. With a mighty shove down that made Cadmus scream aloud, Gellius somersaulted over the top of his opponent's head, springing lightly off Cadmus's neck as though it were a diving board. He landed on his feet with a triumphant flourish and laughed out loud. This was what the Pankration was all about—moves that were clever and so fast people barely had time to observe them. It was a manoeuvre of such grace and agility it took Nic's breath away and made the crowd break into spontaneous applause. Cadmus leapt to his feet too, and they faced each other again, upright. Again they circled once, twice. Cat and mouse, instinct—to the end now.

Cadmus kicked high, both legs off the ground, his left foot fully extended. His foot punched so hard that Gellius's teeth rattled and he followed with a charging elbow that smacked against Gellius's cheek, making his nose pour blood. Gellius reeled and tried to run his tongue over his teeth to see they were all still there. Cadmus spun around behind and locked his elbow over Gellius's neck in a stranglehold.

More than anything Nic wanted to throw himself into the pit and leap on top of Cadmus, pull him off and smash him to a pulp. His blood felt as if it were boiling right inside his veins.

'Gellius!' he shouted. 'Like a reed in the wind!'

That voice carried through the crowd like a golden arrow—it struck its mark precisely. Gellius heard it and remembered that night on the ship, before the pirates had boarded. Somehow he twisted inside the hold, and loosed the pirate's grip on him. Spinning on the ball of his foot like an acrobat, Gellius lithely jumped free and before Cadmus had a chance to take it all in, propelled his knuckles upwards with incredible force, smashing into Cadmus's chin and driving his teeth right through his lips. The pirate reeled backwards and the crowd went wild.

Again the two Pankratiasts sprang onto their feet and circled, a lethal dance around each other. Cadmus feinted and Gellius dodged. Gellius kicked and Cadmus grabbed him by the ankle, pulling his body forward and making him topple over into the mud. Nic watched in horror. Cadmus pressed the advantage. With a single move, he dug his extended fingers directly under the ribs, and with the other hand grasped Gellius's hand, snapping back each finger, one by one in a cruel and deliberate torture. Gellius heard the sound of his own bones, dislocating and breaking. A white-hot agony radiated from his hand all the way up his arm and into the very marrow of his bones, but even worse than the pain was the certain knowledge that this was the end. He had lost.

Among the spectators, screaming and calling for

blood, Nic covered his ears, but he couldn't shut the sound out. He wanted to run away and he wanted to stop this awful fight. Gellius was unrecognisable; covered in streaks of caked-on mud, his hair a tangled, bloody mat.

Cadmus towered over Gellius, who had collapsed, prone and almost unconscious from the pain. In one final insult, the pirate sent his left foot slamming into the captain's genitals.

It was the end.

Cadmus saluted the crowd, while Gellius, unable to get up, raised his good hand in the air in the signal of defeat.

CHAPTER

20

A tangerine-coloured sun dragged itself slowly above the horizon. In a little while it would be too hot for anything more taxing than watching the winners accept their wreaths.

Since before sunrise, a dark-haired boy had been at work in the Altis, and his task was very special. With a little gold sickle, he cut a branch from the sacred olive tree to use for the victors' wreaths. It was important to cut the branch before the dew had left the leaves. The boy twisted the stems into rough crowns, then laid them on the golden table in the temple of Zeus ready for the victory ceremony.

Throughout the Olympic village people were moving about, preparing themselves for the ceremonies. The victors, the losers, the trainers, the judges, the rich and the poor, were bathing and praying and offering up sacrifices to the gods, thanking them for the Games. And all the temples and altars were carefully prepared to accept the homage due to the gods on this final day.

'Are you all right?' Nic spoke in a whisper. The tents around them were still full of men—he didn't want to embarrass the captain.

Gellius nodded. His face was pale and bruised. 'I'm fine. If all I take home with me is a hand full of broken fingers, and a few bruises and cuts then it's better than most. I'll come back for the next Games. You can count on that, young Nic.' He managed a smile. 'And four years from now, when that Olympic moon rises, I expect you to be here competing with me.' Nic nodded, mutely, and tried to smile back, but somehow the idea of competing didn't seem so glorious any more. Not like it had that night on Gellius's boat.

'If I ever compete, it won't be in the Pankration. Maybe running, where I can finish in one piece, and at least I'd stand a chance of winning.'

His friend looked hard at him.

'Winning isn't the reason we come, Nic, we don't compete for our own glory. We do it for the honour of our cities and the glory of our gods. Any man who seeks personal gain in these Games is here for the wrong reasons. I can't pretend that I'm not disappointed, of course I am. I wanted to win, but the gods had other ideas. Now, I have preparations to make. And you should begin to get ready too. We have to attend the crowning ceremony in an hour.' He left the tent to bathe and Nic sat down. He had never felt so crushed and empty in his life.

Porinus came into the tent. 'I heard that,' he said softly. 'You mustn't mind that Gellius didn't win. He tried and that's as much as anyone can ask.' The old trainer shrugged. 'He's pretty philosophical about it. Last time, the loser in the Pankration died. Gellius gets to go home, and everyone knows he put up a good, clean fight. He's not dishonoured here.'

'It's my fault he lost.'

'Ridiculous.' Porinus tried to be cheerful. 'Gellius lost because he's stubborn. That's all. Won't fight dirty, no matter what's at stake. If he'd listened to me, he'd have been better equipped to handle a shabby fighter like that Cadmus. But it didn't matter what I said, he would never do it. He's pigheaded, and that's why he lost.'

It was so hot Nic felt breathless. The crowd outside was already kicking up a dust haze and he felt it was choking him.

'You're wrong. I should have stopped the match altogether. I should have challenged Cadmus when he took the oath.'

'What on earth do you mean?' Porinus stared at Nic as if he were touched in the head.

'He's the pirate who kidnapped me and sold me

165

as a slave! He tried to have me murdered so I wouldn't expose him. He thinks I'm dead!' The whole story of the pirate, Amasis, the stolen money, the cave and the capture tumbled out of Nic's mouth in a torrent of words. When he had finished he looked up miserably.

'So you see, I *am* responsible. I should have stopped the fight.'

Porinus grasped Nic by the shoulder.

'If this is true, then you *must* challenge him.'

'How?' Nic slumped visibly. 'There's absolutely no proof. It'd just be my word against his, and no one's likely to believe me over an Olympic champion, are they?'

'But surely you can identify him.'

'That's just it, I can't. Not absolutely, anyway. I never saw his face, I only saw his feet. He has six toes on his left foot. That's why I know it's him.'

'Six toes!' Porinus sighed. 'Plenty of men might have six toes. You must have noticed something else about him. How else do you know this man is definitely your pirate if you never so much as saw his face?'

'I just know, I don't know how. It's something about him, so vague I can't pick one thing over another. The way he walks, maybe, or the feeling he gives.' Nicasylus tried to remember anything he could about the pirate—what he'd been wearing, what he'd said. 'I remember he didn't sound as if he was from the same place as his crew. He spoke to them in a dialect I couldn't understand and his accent was different to all the others.'

'It sounds as if this rogue has joined himself to a gang of Sardinian pirates. He's probably been making some extra cash by running a few raids close to home where the pickings are good.' Porinus sighed. 'There are plenty of men whose money comes from pain and bloodshed. But you were right not to challenge.' The old trainer began to roll up the animal skins they had been using as beds. 'Without stronger proof, you had better forget it now; there's nothing else to be done.' He tidied up purposefully, as if he were thinking hard. For a few minutes neither spoke.

'It *is* him!' Nic muttered. 'I know it is.'

'Are you positive?' Porinus swung back to Nic. 'Because if you are, then I will challenge for you.'

Nic looked at the ground. He knew just as surely as he knew his own name that Cadmus was the pirate, but it wasn't enough. Porinus had been right the first time. It wouldn't matter who challenged him. It would simply mean that Porinus would be humiliated, and punished for false accusation against a victor in the Games. He shook his head slowly.

'Then let it go, Nicasylus. Or it'll eat away at all of us.'

They got ready for the ceremony in silence.

CHAPTER

21

It took a long time for the crowd to make its way to the Altis. Everywhere a rush of celebration and happiness filled the air. Men were laughing and joking with each other. The athletes stood together in a tight group at the front, proud to even be at the ceremony, whether or not they had won. At the temple of Zeus the procession stopped. Judges, victors, competitors and trainers all made their way inside, and the crowd surged in behind them.

'At least it's cooler in here.' Porinus, leaning on Nic's shoulder, was red in the face. 'I couldn't have taken another step in that sun.' He glanced at the boy. 'Remembered anything yet?'

'No.' Nic wished he could, but there *was* nothing else. From his vantage point near the front, but half hidden by Porinus, he had a perfect view. Despite the protection of the old trainer, Nic was afraid. He tried not to stare at Cadmus, who was standing with other winners in a loose group. Instead he concentrated on watching the purple-robed Hellanodikai as they prepared to award the olive crowns. The victory wreaths lay on the magnificent gold-topped ivory table. There was a sudden hush in the temple.

'Let the victors approach!'

The winners stepped forward solemnly and faced the judges. Cadmus shifted his feet and twisted his fingers together uneasily, as if suddenly, in the face of the gods, he was afraid.

The herald called the first winner.

'Antiphon of Elis, Son of Morsimus, winner in the Hoplite Race.' This was a local winner—it was a very popular result. The man stepped forward and knelt in front of the altar. One of the Hellanodikai placed the olive wreath on top of the thin circlet of wool he already wore to signify his status as a winner. There was a moment of silence before he stood, and then the crowd went wild. Everyone cheered and whistled and he was carried off high on the shoulders of his friends and supporters. The herald called the next name. One by one the victors stepped up and were announced, crowned and carried off in triumph. Nic couldn't keep his eyes off Cadmus now. The man's moment was getting closer and closer. Nic edged forward to get a better view. His head popped through the front of the crowd, and for a split second, he stared right into his enemy's eyes. Cadmus visibly started, and the colour drained from his face. He looked as though he had just seen a ghost.

'Cadmus of Amantia.'

The pirate stepped forward. He looked flustered, and turned to look back at the crowd, but Nic had already hidden himself again.

'Son of Phayllus!' The herald was calling out his parentage. In one short moment the olive crown would lie on his head.

Something flashed right in Nic's eye, so bright it stung. The dream he'd had on the boat to Olympia suddenly came rushing back. '*Gold will save you.*' He could hear the voice in his mind.

'Stop!' Nic darted forward. 'You mustn't crown this man—he's a pirate!'

The effect was spectacular. The Hellanodikai turned as one man towards Nic, and Cadmus staggered backwards in shock. The crowd behind him rumbled with the news; Porinus stood white-faced and Gellius was staring as though he couldn't believe what he was hearing. His eyes were wide with surprise.

'He stole me from the boat I was travelling on, and sold me into slavery.' Nic blurted it out. 'He murdered innocent men.'

'You have proof of this?' A judge had come forward

and now stood in front of Nic, between him and Cadmus.

'I do.'

'What is your proof?'

'Two things.' Nic pointed to the pirate's feet. 'The man who kidnapped me had six toes on his left foot.'

Some people laughed out loud.

'I hope you have better proof than that.' The judges were all looking very grim.

'He's wearing the ring he stole from me.' Nic's finger shot out accusingly. 'There, on his right hand. My stepfather, Gorgias of Athens, made that for me. He gave it to me the night I left Athens. This man took it from me moments before he sold me.'

All eyes had turned back to Cadmus now. His face was white but his eyes still flashed dangerously.

'This ring is mine. What proof does he have that it's his? The kid's a runaway slave, get him out of here!' The pirate covered his little finger with his right hand.

An ominous silence fell over the crowd. Nic felt his heart hammer. His fear was choking him.

'Well? Can you prove the ring is yours?' Cadmus flung out the challenge.

'If Nicasylus, son of Gorgias of Athens, says this is his father's ring, then I say he's right.' Gellius stepped forward. 'I vouch for this boy.'

'And I vouch for this boy.' Porinus stood alongside as well.

A great babble of voices began to speak at once.

'Where *did* you get the ring, Cadmus?' shouted Gellius. His voice carried over the din and the crowd quietened instantly. Every eye was on Cadmus now.

The pirate's eyes were darting rapidly among the sea of faces in front of him.

'It's true this ring was made by Gorgias.' His face smoothed into a smile. 'I bought it from him!'

'You're lying!' Nic leapt forward and stood right in front of Cadmus. 'You were never in my stepfather's shop!'

'Someone take this idiot away.' Cadmus was losing his temper. He shoved Nic hard, in the chest with the flat of his hand and Nic sprawled backwards.

'Enough!' One of the judges stepped between the two of them. 'You are claiming victory in the sacred Games, and as such you are sworn to be peaceful.' He helped Nic to his feet. 'We will hear from the boy.'

Nic tried to swallow, but his throat was dry. The Hellanodikai were all looking at him.

'Your history, please.'

'Whatever he says, it's a lie!' Cadmus interjected loudly. 'He's a beggar. Not the son of some jeweller in Athens.'

'Not just *some* jeweller, the *best* jeweller.' Gellius's voice was clear, and it carried. 'How long ago did you buy this ring from Gorgias, Cadmus? Can you tell us?'

Cadmus paused a moment too long. He looked

rattled. 'Oh, many years ago,' he stammered. 'Five or more.'

'Are you quite sure?' Gellius was smiling now, widely and openly. 'Only five years ago?'

'I'm not sure, maybe it was six.' The pirate was frantically twisting the ring on his finger. 'Yes. Yes. It *was* six. I'm sure.'

Gellius faced the Hellanodikai. He pointed at Cadmus.

'There is the proof you need. I saw this boy wearing that ring, on board my ship, just before she was raided by pirates.'

'Even so—' The judge began.

There was a sudden commotion from the rear of the crowd. Someone was pushing a way forward, shouting. It wasn't till he got close that Nic could make out what he was saying.

'I can prove the boy's story! I can prove it! Let me through!'

The man walked right up to Nic and kissed him on the cheek.

'Welcome, Nicasylus. I am Diagoras of Argos, your uncle. And this man'—Diagoras faced the pirate—'is lying.'

Nic was astonished. He stared at his uncle and it was as if he saw his stepfather, Gorgias, looking back at him. They were so alike.

'He's lying, and I can prove it. Make him give me

the ring so that I can see it properly.'

Cadmus looked around uneasily. He tried to smile.

'By all means look at the ring. It's mine, I bought it.' He thrust the gold ring into Diagoras's hand. Diagoras turned the ring over and examined it carefully.

'This ring is not one that my brother would ever have sold,' he announced loudly. 'It is not something he made himself. This is our great-grandfather's ring, made by him and given to the eldest son in each generation since. It belonged to Gorgias, and he would have given it only to his eldest son. I've been waiting for this boy since my brother sent him out of Athens when the plague first began. He never arrived. This belongs to you, Nicasylus.' Diagoras handed the ring to Nic.

There was a sudden flurry of noise and Cadmus sprang forward. He grabbed Nic and wrapped one huge arm around his throat in a stranglehold. 'That ring is mine! Everything this boy has said is a lie! I won't let him ruin this day for me. I've waited too long. I won the Pankration! I'm an Olympic champion and no one is going to change that.'

Guards had begun to advance on him, menacingly.

'Keep away, or the boy dies!' Still squeezing against Nic's throat, Cadmus backed away slowly. Nic struggled like a demon in the man's grip, but he was trapped.

Above the noise of the crowd Porinus shouted, 'An

Olympic victor wins for his country and his gods, not himself. The olive crown isn't earned by strength alone, it's earned by truth and fairness. You insult Zeus himself by claiming this wreath.'

'I earned it, it's mine!' Cadmus backed up to the table and grabbed an olive crown from the gold top. He held it aloft in his free hand, ranting as he did.

'I crown myself winner of the Pankration!'

A giant rabbit punch landed on the back of the pirate's neck and felled him like a stone. Nic rubbed his neck and turned to see what had happened. Behind him stood Gellius, a silly grin on his face.

'Well, Gellius.' Porinus was chuckling. 'That was a dirty punch if I ever saw one. I didn't think I'd live to see the day.'

'It surprised me too.' Gellius was rubbing his fist. 'But it felt good! Just as well I had one useful hand left.'

Cadmus was dragged from the temple by six guards. They held his arms behind him and pushed his head towards the ground with heavy hands. The crowd roared with anger and the pirate was buffeted and shoved all the way out, like unwanted vermin. Outside, the men with whips were ready.

'Gellius! There's a thief tied up in a cave near the river Cladeus.' Nic suddenly remembered Amasis. 'Cadmus paid him to murder me so I couldn't denounce him. He's been there for a day and a half. Someone should fetch him soon.'

'He'll be dealt with along with your pirate, lad,' Porinus said. 'But before we bother with him, there's something we need to witness here.'

The Hellanodikai had ushered Gellius to the front. The herald called out his name.

'Victor in the Pankration! Gellius of Athens, son of Hermes.' The olive wreath descended on the captain's head and an incredible shout went up. People were calling his name and he was lifted onto shoulders, high above the crowd; he was laughing and crying at once.

'Nic!' he called. 'This is for your father and mine. This is for both of us!'

Then the crowd hoisted Nic as well, as if he were no more than a feather, till he was head and shoulders above the sea of faces.

A feeling such as he had never had before surged through Nic. The roar of the crowd, the approval and the honour, the love and admiration of thousands of men swept over him and he was weak with it. This was better than anything he'd ever known. He heard Gellius's voice across the sea of sound and men.

'Four years from now, Nicasylus. You and me. A runner and a Pankratiast—is it a promise?'

Laughter and tears mingled.

'It's a promise.'

Nothing could stop him now.

HISTORICAL NOTE

In 430 BC, Athens was struck by a terrible plague. It couldn't have come at a worse time. Athens had been at war with neighbouring Sparta for a year. The city was full to overflowing with refugees from the nearby countryside, who had poured in, looking for refuge behind the city's walls. There was severe overcrowding everywhere and hygiene was poor, so rats would have been plentiful. Historians do not agree about what caused this plague, or even what it was. One theory has it that it was a terrible strain of measles, another that it was pneumonic plague, another that it was a sickness transmitted virally from Ethiopia. There is also the possibility that it was caused by the fleas from infected rats, and I have followed this theory. Whatever the cause, the outcome was devastating; about a quarter of the population died, and for many

177

families, life was never the same.

Wherever possible, this story is historically accurate, but I have used my imagination freely. Authors are allowed to do this, and anyway, I don't think history should stand in the way of a terrific story.